F
MAR   Marcantonio, Patri-
         cia Santos

         Red ridin' in the
         hood

                        0705 16.00
DUE DATE

Red Ridin' in the Hood

Red Ridin' in the Hood

and Other *Cuentos*

Patricia Santos Marcantonio

Pictures by **Renato Alarcão**

Farrar Straus Giroux
New York

For Manuel and Connie,

the best storytellers,

the best parents

—P.S.M.

Distributed in Canada by Douglas & McIntyre Publishing Group
Printed in the United States of America
Designed by Jay Colvin
First edition, 2005
1   3   5   7   9   10   8   6   4   2

www.fsgkidsbooks.com

Library-of-Congress Cataloging-in-Publication Data

Marcantonio, Patricia Santos.
    Red ridin' in the hood : and other cuentos / Patricia Santos Marcantonio ; pictures by
Renato Alarcão.— 1st ed.
        p. cm.
    Summary: A collection of well-known tales, retold from a Hispanic American perspective.
    Contents: Jaime and Gabriela — Red ridin' in the hood — Blanca Nieves and the seven
vaqueritos — El día de los muertos — Juan and the pinto bean stalk — The piper of
Harmonía — Alejandro and the spirit of the magic lámpara — Belleza y la Bestia —
Emperador's new clothes — The three chicharrones — The sleeping beauty.
    ISBN-13: 978-0-374-36241-6
    ISBN-10: 0-374-36241-6

    1. Fairy tales—United States. 2. Children's stories, American. [1. Fairy tales. 2. Hispanic
Americans—Fiction. 3. Short stories.] I. Title: Red riding in the hood. II. Alarcão, Renato,
ill. III. Title.

PZ8.M334Re 2005
[Fic]—dc22

                                                                                      2004043331

Contents

Red Ridin' in the Hood

Jaime and Gabriela

TIMES WERE POOR FOR THE ADOBE MAKER and his family, who found themselves living in a desert of *nopales*, scorpions, and despair.

In fact, the whole village, once a place of great bounty, was troubled. Chickens laid rocks, cornstalks broke like straw, wells dried to a whisper, and cows gave curdled milk. Even the apple trees drooped with sadness.

"A *bruja* has put a curse on the place," people whispered in the market and after church. The townsfolk prayed hard to La Virgen de Guadalupe to remove the evil they felt sure was caused by an unknown witch in their midst—a witch who carried a grudge against the village. They could think of no other reason for these sorrowful days.

Naturally, no one wanted new bricks, for there was no reason to build anything. Francisco the adobe maker dreaded coming home at the end of each day with only sorrow. His second wife would not let him forget his failure to find work.

This day was no different. "*Hombre*, you are worthless! We have nothing to eat," she yelled. "*¡Nada!*"

The adobe maker felt worse for his children, Jaime and Gabriela, who went to bed with stomachs growling like mountain lions. They had always been poor, even before these hard times, but they were rich in spirit. They didn't complain and always smiled, just like their mother, who had died when they were babies.

"Maybe tomorrow you will find work, Papi," Jaime said, bringing him a cup of weak coffee.

"I know you will soon sell some bricks. They are the best in the country," Gabriela said, holding his rough hand.

"Go to bed," the wife ordered, and kissed each child on the cheek. Her lips were cracked as a thirsty riverbed; she puckered them as if eating a rotten lemon.

Jaime sensed something bad was going to happen. Madrasta, as they called their second mother, had never kissed him or his sister before.

The boy always wanted to ask Madrasta why she did not love him and Gabriela. They tried their best to be good, but their stepmother said they were ungrateful children. And those words hurt worse than a slap. So he just said, "*Buenas noches*, Madrasta."

After the children went to bed, the wife threw open the pantry door.

"Just look, Francisco. We only have a few beans, one skinny *conejo*, and three tortillas to eat," she told the adobe maker.

The noise woke Jaime and Gabriela, who crawled out of their straw bed to listen through their bedroom door.

The wife slid closer to her husband and said hoarsely, "Tomorrow, when we gather wild grass for your bricks, we shall take the children and leave them in the desert. If we keep having to feed them as well as ourselves, we'll all die."

Francisco stood up. "I will not abandon my children."

"You must!" Then the wife turned soft and touched his hand. "Do you want to see them starve? Do you want to watch them waste away to bones and fingers? If we leave them in the desert, they will be in God's hands, and that will be a blessing."

The adobe maker wept, and Madrasta knew she would have her way, wicked though it was.

Jaime and Gabriela crept back to bed.

"What do we do, *hermano*?" Gabriela shivered under the rags that were their bedclothes.

"I will think of something. Go to sleep, *chiquilla*."

When the house was silent and the moon high as a dream, Jaime left his bed, went outside, and collected some small stones that shone in the moonlight like jeweled rosary beads. He placed them in a little bag.

5

"Wake up." Madrasta shook them in their bed the next morning. "To-day, you will come with your father and me. Here's your breakfast."

She handed them each half of a dried corn tortilla.

"It's time to go, *mis hijos*," their father said gently, but he would not look into their faces.

As they walked, Jaime dropped the shiny pebbles behind him. Gabriela smiled and squeezed his hand.

In the shade of a tall saguaro, Madrasta ordered the children to rest, while she and their father went in search of wild grass.

Their father kissed the top of their heads. "I love you, *hijos*."

"*Vámonos*, Francisco," Madrasta commanded.

6

Gabriela nibbled on the tortilla as she watched her father and Madrasta gather the brittle grass, but she soon fell asleep in her brother's arms. Jaime, too, eventually nodded off.

When they woke, Jaime and Gabriela were in darkness. The moon was like the yellow eye of a monster.

Gabriela cried, "Jaime, they've really left us! We'll be eaten by wild animals."

"No, sister. *¡Mira!*" He pointed to the shiny rocks he had dropped on the way. "These will lead us home."

When morning came, they were in their beds. Their father kissed them, joy in his tired eyes.

Madrasta frowned at the sight of the children.

"How dare you wander off like that yesterday. Now, go do your work," she ordered. And that was all she said to Jaime and Gabriela all day until it was time to go to sleep.

"Good night, Papi. Good night, Madrasta," the children said as they went to bed.

Later, Jaime and Gabriela woke to the sound of Madrasta's voice.

"Francisco, we must take them out even farther into the desert."

"No! Their return was a sign from el Señor." The adobe maker pointed to heaven.

The second wife forced out a tear. "My husband, it is the only way. They will live in *el cielo* as angels—never to be hungry again."

The adobe maker stood. "In the morning, I am going to the next town to see if I can sell my bricks. God gave us another chance to be good."

Then he went to bed, while Madrasta hummed to herself, a song only she knew.

"Jaime, do not worry. We are safe." Gabriela yawned.

"Just in case, I will get more shiny pebbles," he replied.

When the moon rose later that night, the boy tiptoed to the door but found it locked. He shivered with the cold of fear and frustration.

The next morning, their father left very early. Jaime and Gabriela fed measly bits of grain to the chickens and sang to them in hopes they would lay something besides rocks.

Madrasta called to the children, "We are going to find grass for your father's bricks. Here is half of a tortilla. Don't eat it all now or you'll be hungry later."

"But Madrasta—" Jaime started to say.

"Quiet. Don't you want to help your father?" Madrasta's smile was thin and frightening.

So off they went. Gabriela held tight to her brother's hand. Jaime winked, for he was dropping bits of his tortilla behind him so they could follow the trail home.

After they had traveled a long distance, Madrasta pointed to a tall yucca plant. "Rest there. I will be back soon."

Jaime and Gabriela closed their eyes. Sleep came easily because they'd had nothing to eat. Their tortilla was on the trail.

When they awakened, the sun had already slipped from the sky. Gabriela again cried that they were lost.

"No, no . . ." Jaime said, but his mouth turned down as he saw a mouse take away the last bit of tortilla and, with it, the chance of finding the way home.

Gabriela cried harder. Jaime held her close and told her not to worry. He sang her a hymn they had learned in church.

The next morning, they searched for home, and the next and the next, eating piñon nuts and sucking water out of cactuses, for a desert has no pity.

"Jaime, *tengo hambre.*" Gabriela rubbed her empty belly.

He put his arm around her. "I know, *chiquilla.*"

Then the shadow of a shiny black crow crossed over Jaime's face. One of its wings curled, and the bird dipped as if pointing the way to something.

Jaime shaded his eyes with his hand. "That *cuervo* wants us to go over there, Gabriela."

"But crows are evil, remember, Jaime?"

"That's an old wives' tale. Let's go."

They hurried until they reached a small house. But it was no ordinary house.

Surrounded by desert willow trees, the house was made all of *pan dulce*—round, perfect sweet breads, topped by sugars of many colors. The roof tiles were tamales—plump, steaming, spicy, and inviting.

"Are we in heaven, *hermano*?" Gabriela asked.

"I don't know where we are," he said. "But I've never seen so much food in one place."

They ran to the house and stuffed bits of the wall into their mouths, then climbed up a tree and ate some tamales. Their stomachs grew full and sore because they had forgotten what it was like to eat more than half a tortilla. They grabbed their middles and moaned, but smiled and kept eating, afraid the house would disappear like rain in the desert.

"Who is eating *mi casa dulce*?" rattled a voice.

Jaime and Gabriela stopped in mid-bite. Out of the door came a woman wrinkled like time, her hair in white braids; she was walking with a cane made from the thighbone of a horse. They took a step back, but the woman smiled.

"*Pobrecitos, pobrecitos.* Come inside, I will give you something better to eat than my house," she said.

"*Gracias, señora.*" The children bowed.

Inside, the *casa dulce* was neat and smelled of fresh bread. Gabriela also noticed another odor, which she couldn't recognize and made her uneasy.

From a wall filled with hanging *hierbas* of all kinds, the old woman cut pieces of a dried chamomile flower and began to boil water.

Surely, this was a wonderful place for cooking, with its many large pots and pans. But most wondrous was the mud-brick oven. It was as large as an outbuilding, with an iron door as tall as a man.

"You are lost, no?" the woman said.

The children nodded.

"Times are hard, and children often are lost and hungry. Sit, children, sit." She pointed to a table and chairs.

Before them she placed large bowls of *menudo*, a spicy stew of hominy and tripe, and stacks of tortillas the size of wheels. They ate and ate.

"You may call me Sombra, *niños*," the old woman said, grinding herbs in her stone *molcajete*.

12

When they were so full they could barely move, Sombra led them to a featherbed in another room so they could sleep. But throughout the night, Jaime turned and turned like a worm caught by the large *cuervo* that had guided them to Sombra's house. He dreamed of sweet breads that nibbled at him and of hell's fire in the big oven.

Someone grabbed his arm the next morning. It was Sombra.

"Mi comida," she chanted over and over as she dragged Jaime outside and threw him into a cage. This cage was made not of *pan dulce* but of steel and sinfulness. Gabriela begged Sombra to free her brother. But the woman turned the key to the big lock and placed it on a string around her neck.

The *viejita* pointed a scrawny finger at Jaime. "I will fatten you up and eat you for my dinner, because nothing tastes so good as a chubby little boy."

She turned to Gabriela. "You will help me cook for your brother. As a reward, I will eat you last."

Over the next few days, Gabriela's tears went into every dish they cooked for Jaime—and there were many: chicken with *mole* sauce, made from chilies and chocolate; *arroz* with large chunks of goat meat; burritos as round as their father's arm.

"Why do you eat children, Señora Sombra?" Gabriela asked while they made chorizo and eggs.

Sombra scratched her hairy chin. "They keep me young. I am two hun-

13

dred years old, so I stay alive by eating their youth. Children also taste of innocence and sweetness—that is something grown people lose through the years."

The *viejita* grinned, showing her yellow teeth. "Tomorrow, I shall gobble down your brother and his youth so that I will look only *one* hundred years old."

That night, Gabriela sneaked out to see her brother. "What shall we do? Sombra wants to eat you."

"I cannot help, Gabriela. You alone can save us."

"I will try, Jaime."

They held hands through the bars and prayed for strength and an idea that would free them both.

That night in her bed, Gabriela thought of the great oven, and a plan grew in her mind like a grain of wheat gone wild—it grew into hope.

The old woman readied her pans the next morning, clanking them, banging them together.

"If you *must* cook my brother," Gabriela said to the *viejita*, "I know how to make a chili that he loves to eat. That is the way he would like to be cooked."

Sombra licked her lips with her snakelike tongue. "You are a good girl. I will chew slowly when it is your turn."

"Gracias." Gabriela bowed.

Gabriela told Sombra how much onion, cumin, and lard to add. "The oven must be very, very hot so that he will cook well."

Sombra threw in logs. Although the heat curled the ends of her hair, Gabriela said, "That is not hot enough."

"Girl, are you stupid? This is hot enough for anything." Sombra opened the oven, the heat almost knocking her back.

"It needs to be even hotter for the best meal you will ever eat," Gabriela said.

"See, I will show you, silly girl." The *viejita* leaned close to the flames. "It couldn't get any hotter."

Gabriela took a breath, grabbed the key from Sombra's neck, and pushed the old woman into the oven. She slammed the door shut, praying for forgiveness, even though Sombra was a sister of sin.

Outside, Jaime watched a red fireball shoot out from the chimney and into the sky.

Gabriela freed her brother, and they hugged. "You are smart and brave, *mi hermana*. You have saved me," he said.

"But how do we get home, brother?"

"I'm not sure, but for now, we have each other and our lives."

While Gabriela gathered food to take with them, Jaime searched the rest of the *casa*. He spotted a plain-looking box under Sombra's bed. The glow when he opened it blinded him for a moment. Inside were gold coins. He and Gabriela stared at the box for a long time and then packed up many coins, but not all.

"Let's leave some money for the next lost children," Gabriela said. Her brother agreed.

At sunrise the next day, they set off into the desert, picking a way that felt as if it was leading them home. That night, they rested near a large cactus, and were protected under its spiny arms.

When the sky was again orange with morning, a dove fluttered above them.

"A *paloma blanca.*" Gabriela smiled. The dove banked and seemed to summon them. "It is leading us home."

They followed, and at last they saw the houses and church of their village. But much had changed. The trees were full and colored with apples and pears. Cows mooed, asking for people to milk them. Young girls gathered eggs in baskets, and women sang as they drew water from wells.

Jaime and Gabriela felt as if they could fly like the dove, which flapped its wings and sailed in the sky. They ran home. When their father saw them, he fell to his knees and kissed their faces.

"Where is Madrasta?" Jaime asked.

"She died one night in a burst of red fire," their father replied. "The next day, the village came back to life. I believe it was she who had put the curse on the place with her hatefulness and selfishness."

The children presented the gold to their father, telling him of Sombra and the big oven at the *casa dulce.*

"We never will be poor, Papi," Gabriela said.

But their father's face was sorrowful. "Forgive me for being weak and not taking better care of you."

"Papi, as long as we have each other, we will never be lost again," Jaime said.

Then the children hugged their father as tight as they could, and he knew he had been forgiven.

Red Ridin' in the Hood

INSIDE A CARDBOARD BOX, Mamá packed a tin of chicken soup, heavy on cilantro, along with a jar of peppermint tea, peppers from our garden, and a hunk of white goat cheese that smelled like Uncle José's feet.

That meant one thing.

"Roja, your *abuelita* is not feeling well," Mamá told me. "I want you to take this food to her."

"But Mamá, me and Lupe Maldonado are going to the movies," I replied, but felt guilty as soon as I'd said it.

"What's more important? Your grandmother or Lupe and the movies?" Mamá closed up the box.

"Wear your new red dress, the one that Abuelita made for you. That will make her feel better," Mamá said.

I couldn't say no because I didn't want to feel guilty again, so I put on the red dress. It was long and old-fashioned, with a high collar. I looked like the kid on *Little House on the Prairie*.

"Go straight to Abuelita's apartment," Mamá said.

"*Sí*, Mamá," I answered.

"Here's bus fare."

"*Sí*, Mamá."

"And keep away from Forest Street. You know it means trouble."

"*Sí*, Mamá."

I waited for another order, but instead Mamá kissed my cheek.

The day was bright, so I put on my sunglasses, hoping none of my friends would see me carrying a cardboard box that smelled like Uncle José's feet and wearing a dress that made me look *estúpida*.

I decided to walk and keep the bus fare. I was saving change for a new shirt I had seen in the window of the Martínez clothing store—a shirt a whole lot cooler than the number I was wearing.

After a few blocks, my arms grew tired carrying the box and I knew I needed to take a shortcut. I looked up. There it was.

FOREST STREET.

I could hear Mamá's voice telling me to stay away, but I didn't listen.

Forest Street got its name because it was lined with the biggest trees in the whole barrio, tall and thick and blocking out the sun, making even morning light seem like sunset. As I walked down the street, the city and

home seemed far away. Birds whistled a delicate, carefree rhythm. Two skinny police officers nodded to me as they walked past.

"I don't know why Mamá says this block is trouble," I said to myself. "It's quiet and kinda peaceful."

But as I walked farther, the trees grew thicker and Forest Street grew dark.

Then came a roar and the blare of loud salsa music.

Up rolled a glossy brown low-rider Chevy with licks of flame painted on the hood. It jolted up and down, the hydraulics making the driver's large, hairy ears bounce. His smile was broad and full of teeth. SUAVECITO was painted on the back windshield in blue and silver.

"*¡Hola!*" he greeted me.

I didn't stop. I remembered Mamá's advice about not talking to strangers, and this guy was strange.

"I say, *hola*, Red."

I stopped. "How'd you know my name?"

"You're wearing red, ain't you?" His smile and laugh were mixed with a growl. "My name is Lobo, Lobo Chávez."

I began walking again.

"Where you going?" He pushed his sunglasses to the top of his head. His eyes were orange hungry marbles.

"Not that it's any of your business, Lobo Chávez, but I'm going to visit my *abuelita*. She's not feeling so well today."

"You should be careful," he said. "Lots of bad dudes hanging around Forest Street."

"Like you?"

"Not me. I'm harmless." Lobo's gigantic tongue went all the way around his mouth and over his large black nose. "Hey, Roja, just a few doors down is the best *panadería* in town. Stop in and get your *abuelita* some empanadas with *calabaza*. She'll love 'em."

"Thank you. I will."

Lobo pulled down his sunglasses. "I hope your ol' grandma feels better, Red." He zoomed up the street, hydraulics in time to the beat of the music on his radio.

Lobo Chávez was right about the bakery. The *calabaza* empanadas were great. I bought two, one for Abuelita and one for me, which I ate as I walked slowly, enjoying the treat. But then I noticed the sun starting to go down, so I hurried.

Abuelita's apartment building was at the edge of Forest Street. I ran up the stairs and knocked at her door.

No answer.

"Abuelita, it's Roja."

Inside, I heard scurrying.

"Abuelita, are you okay?"

"*Sí*, Roja. *Entra*," a little voice said.

The room smelled of the lavender soap my grandma used. It also

25

smelled like wet dog. That was unusual because Abuelita's landlord wouldn't let her have a pet.

"I'm in the bedroom, Roja," she called to me.

"Abuelita, you sound like you got a chest cold."

I opened the door. The shades were drawn and the room was dark. But there was enough light to see Lobo Chávez in Abuelita's bed, wearing her nightgown and glasses and smiling as if I didn't notice he was not my grandmother.

I knew then that this was one pretty dumb wolf.

Yet I worried he might have hurt my grandmother. I realized suddenly how much I really loved her, and how angry I was at this wolf in Abuelita's clothing. I decided to play along to find out what had happened to her.

"Abuelita, look at what Mamá sent you," I said, all cheery, like the girl on *Little House*, and set the food on the table.

"That looks so good." Lobo rubbed his bloated stomach.

I wanted to laugh, but couldn't.

"Abuelita, I never noticed before, but what big *orejas* you have."

He put a hand to his ear. "The better to hear you with, *nieta*."

"And what big *ojos* you have, Abuelita," I said.

"The better to see you with, Roja." Lobo opened his eyes so big I thought they would pop out of his head.

"And, Abuelita, what big *dientes* you have."

Lobo slobbered a little. He had been waiting for this one. He leaped out of my grandmother's bed. "The better to eat you with!"

26

But I had secretly grabbed a chunk of the goat cheese, and when Lobo opened his big mouth, I shoved in the whole smelly piece.

Lobo put his claws to his throat and groaned. "This tastes like someone's dirty feet. Yuck!"

I ran out the door and yelled, "POLICE!"

The two officers I had passed earlier ran up the stairs.

"That wolf has my grandmother," I told them.

The officers chased Lobo around the apartment, but the wolf tripped on Abuelita's long nightgown, and they easily caught him.

"Where is my grandmother, Lobo Chávez?" I yelled.

"She wasn't here. I was going to eat you and then eat her for dessert when she came home. I eat people. That's my job," Lobo confessed, his face still a little green from eating all that stinky cheese.

Just then, Abuelita walked in.

"Where have you been?" I hugged my grandmother. "A wolf was going to eat us."

"I was feeling better and went out for a quick game of bingo," she said.

Abuelita looked at Lobo. "Officers, please take my nightgown off that wolf. He's getting hair all over it."

"Yes, *señora*," the officers replied.

"Well, I'm happy you are safe, Abuelita," I said.

"And I am happy *you* are safe," she said. "This is a dangerous world, and it's best to keep your eyes and ears wide open, even if they aren't as big as a wolf's."

"Good advice." One of the officers smiled. "We are taking this Lobo Chávez to jail for planning to eat people and impersonating a little old lady. We'll lock him up until his teeth fall out and the only thing he can eat is oatmeal."

The wolf howled.

"Here you go, young lady. You deserve this for your bravery." The police officer threw me the keys to Lobo's low-rider.

The wolf howled again.

"Come on, you." The officers took Lobo Chávez away.

"Well, I'm hungry after all this excitement," Abuelita said. "What did you bring me?"

"Chicken soup and peppers, and the goat cheese that saved our lives," I said.

"Is that the *queso* that smells like your Uncle José's feet?"

"Yes."

Abuelita grabbed her sweater. "How about Chinese, Roja?"

"I'd love it, Abuelita. And I love you."

Off we went in my new low-rider. We both laughed as hydraulics bumped us along, and I never had to walk down Forest Street again.

29

Blanca Nieves and the Seven Vaqueritos

BLANCA NIEVES LOVED TO RIDE HER HORSE over the lands of her father's *rancho*. She loved the delicate smell of the sagebrush and how the rain made the grass shine like jade.

She was a happy young woman, but would have been happier if her mother had lived long enough to go riding with her and see her grow up. Her mother had died the day she was born, during an unusual snowfall for the region, so she was named Blanca Nieves.

Blanca stopped to let her horse drink at a pond. Her father, Avi, had told her that she looked just like her mother, with long black hair down her back, deep brown eyes, and skin the color of earth. Blanca saw her reflection in the water and pretended it *was* her mother standing there, smiling at her.

"Mamá, isn't it a beautiful day?" she whispered at the reflection, which smiled back.

Blanca galloped home. Her father was returning that day after being away for a long time to buy new horses, and she counted the hoofbeats back to him as she got closer and closer to their *rancho*.

"Blanca!" her father shouted when he saw her riding through the gate.

"I missed you," she called, and they hugged. Beside her father was a handsome woman, with a face like the statue of a saint but with eyes cold as marble.

Her father took the hand of the woman. "Blanca, this is your new stepmother, Malvina."

Blanca hugged the woman, who felt as stiff as dry wood. "You must be tired. Welcome to our hacienda, Malvina."

"*Gracias*, my dear Blanca. I know I'll be very happy here."

Blanca and her father did not know that Malvina really was spiteful, vain, and only cared about herself and money. The woman would admire her beauty for hours in the mirror or anything else that reflected her face. In the days to come, Malvina grew jealous of Blanca's goodness and beauty and of her husband's love for his daughter. She also desired all of his wealth and property.

So Malvina planned and planned, schemed and schemed, her mind like a wheel that never stopped turning. Then the wheel halted when she came up with a plot. She summoned her old servant, Carlos, who had come with her to live on the *rancho*.

"Carlos," Malvina told him that night, "Blanca will go riding tomorrow."

"*Sí*, Blanca always goes riding in the morning, Doña Malvina."

"I want you to follow her—follow her and kill her."

Carlos stepped back and shook his head. "Doña Malvina, she's but an innocent young woman."

Malvina pretended to cry. Someone with no soul can pretend to cry very easily. "Blanca wants me dead. She wants this *rancho* all to herself." Malvina touched his hand. "*Por favor*, Carlos. You'll be saving my life if you take hers."

Then she handed him a gold box. "And bring me her heart in this."

Carlos reluctantly agreed, but the decision sat with him like a bad meal.

The next day, Blanca kissed her father and Malvina goodbye before she went on her ride.

"Be careful," her father said, his voice full of love.

"*¡Adiós!*" Malvina wore the deceptive smile of the wicked.

Carlos followed at a distance, waiting for the right moment. At last, Blanca led her horse into an arroyo so it could drink.

Carlos rode up.

"*Buenos días.*" Blanca waved.

He stepped from his horse and drew his knife. Blanca saw it shine as he raised the blade tight in his fist above her.

"Your stepmother said that you are evil and must die, *señorita*."

But Blanca didn't scream or show fear.

33

"May I first say my prayers and make a confession of my sins?" Blanca said.

Carlos nodded. Her bravery moved him. The knife handle felt clammy in his hand.

Without a tear, Blanca sank to her knees. "Please, God," she prayed, "bless and watch over my father and please forgive Carlos and my step-mother."

Carlos let his hand drop to his side. He knew he had been used by Doña Malvina. "Forgive me, Señorita Blanca. Your stepmother is the one who is evil. She's jealous of you, and she wants you dead." Just then, he spotted an antelope grazing nearby.

34

"I will kill that animal and tell your stepmother that it is your blood I spilled. Please, do not return home," Carlos ordered.

Blanca got on her horse and rode away. Above her, the clouds grew dark and swollen with rain. She rode with no place to go, leaving her father's love behind her like a shadow. Needles of rain stung her face, but there was little refuge on the flat grasslands. At last, she stopped under a young cot-tonwood tree. There were puddles all around, and she hoped to see her mother's reflection in the water to comfort her.

"*¿Dónde estás*, Mamá? Where are you? And where can I go?"

But the rain distorted her reflection. Blanca hid under the tree and cried out of desperation until she fell asleep.

When she awoke, however, she was not alone.

Standing around her were seven small *vaqueros*, no taller than her waist.

"Hola, vaqueritos," she greeted them.

They took off their sombreros and bowed.

"Are you hurt, *señorita?*" said one *vaquerito*, whose voice was as high as he was short.

"No, *señor*, but I am lost."

"You're also wet and hungry. Come to our *rancho*," said another *vaquerito*.

Grateful, Blanca rode with the little men, who also had little horses.

RANCHO GARCÍA read the sign on the gate to their house, which was made of logs. Blanca had to stoop to get in the front door. Inside, the house smelled of cumin from a big pot of green chili on the stove. The *vaqueritos* chatted among themselves, their tiny voices sounding like birds. After dinner, they brought out a huge jar of chokecherry jam and spread it on thick slices of bread. They all sat back and listened as Blanca told them her story.

"Then you must live with us, where you will be safe," said one of the little cowboys. "But forgive me and my brothers for not introducing ourselves. We are the *hermanos* García. I am Lazo because I am good with a rope."

"Mi nombre es Cacto," another said without a smile.

"He's always like that," Lazo whispered to Blanca. "Prickly like a cactus."

A brother who had a long face said, "I am Caballo. I am better with a horse than all my brothers."

The other brothers shook their heads in disagreement.

36

"Toro is my name." This one stood up and showed his muscles. "I am strong as a bull."

"And as stubborn!" his brothers shouted.

Another brother had silver buttons on his vest, silver spurs on his boots, silver rings on his fingers, and even a silver tooth. "You can see why they call me Plateado."

"Yes, I can see why," Blanca said.

"Cocinero at your service, *señorita*. I love to cook for my brothers."

"And I am Paco. I am the bookkeeper for our *rancho*."

"I am very happy to meet you all," Blanca said. "I would love to stay with you, but you must let me help out if I do."

"Can you cook?" Cacto said gruffly. "Cocinero is a terrible cook." 37

"What!" Cocinero said. "I thought you liked my beef-brain burritos with cinnamon."

"I am sorry to say that I am a bad cook," Blanca said, "but I have been around horses all my life and can help on the *rancho*."

"*Qué rancherita*, ha!" Plateado waved his silver ring–covered hands.

"I am strong and will work hard," Blanca replied.

"Let her work," Lazo argued. "Besides, she is bigger than all of us and will get twice as much done."

Blanca laughed, and the *vaqueritos* laughed with her.

The next months were good ones for the brothers, who came to love Blanca. To them she was as gentle and refreshing as a summer day. And Blanca came to love the *vaqueritos* in return.

Each night after supper, while they cleaned dishes, the brothers told stories. Often they were about vengeful witches and ghosts who were ready to snatch a person's soul down to the underworld.

"Blanca, it is for that reason that you should never talk to strangers," Cacto warned her one night.

"Yes, I understand," she said, warmed by their care and devotion to her.

Still, as happy as she was, Blanca missed her father. She longed for home, which now seemed like a distant land.

One day, as Blanca helped the brothers gather up cattle, Toro noticed that a calf had gone missing.

"I'll find it," Blanca yelled to him, and rode off toward the gully. She guessed that the little calf had been thirsty, and she found it near a pond, mooing for his mother, stuck in the mud.

"There you are, little *vaca*." Blanca pulled it out of the mud, and the calf lowed gratefully.

Before getting back on her horse, Blanca paused to stare at her image in the water. Her face was dirty, and in her sombrero she could be mistaken for a boy. She took off the large hat, and her dark, thick hair fell down her back. She splashed water on her face. Now she looked more like a girl, like her mother, young and hopeful. But the water also showed a stranger behind her.

Blanca spun around, and there was a young man. He took off his own large sombrero respectfully.

"I didn't mean to frighten you," he said. His voice was like a night breeze, comforting and friendly.

"Who are you?"

"Oscar Huerta." He pointed into the distance. "Our *rancho* is over there. Excuse me, but I had to stop when I saw you."

"Why?"

"I thought you were a beautiful guardian angel because you seemed to make even the water shine with goodness."

She blushed at the compliment. "I'm just a girl. My name is Blanca."

Oscar's face reminded her of her father's, full of strength and sincerity. Then she remembered the brothers' warnings about strangers.

"I must go." She hopped onto her horse.

"No, wait . . ."

Blanca stayed a moment longer.

"I'm glad you're real," Oscar said.

Blanca rode away, still seeing Oscar's face in her mind.

• • •

Meanwhile, at Blanca's *rancho*, her father had sent men all over his many hectares of land and even to the surrounding hills in search of his daughter. The more they looked, the more he despaired he would never see his beloved Blanca again. Had she been killed by a mountain lion? Had she fallen and died alone on the range? His loss was as vast as the sky.

"I miss my Blanca Nieves," he told his wife.

"There, there, *mi esposo*," Malvina told him, faking her tears in the open but laughing in private. "I'll go to the chapel and pray we find your child."

Malvina's plan was so simple. The *rancho* was half hers already, and when her husband died—early, with her help—she would own it all. Such were her thoughts as she walked by the large copper-framed mirror in the hallway. Malvina stopped, never passing up an opportunity to look at herself. But this time, instead of her own face, she saw Blanca's, more beautiful than ever before. Blanca stood in front of a gate with a sign that read RANCHO GARCÍA.

Malvina's face became gnarled with anger. *So Carlos hadn't killed the girl, after all,* she thought. *She would just have to find Blanca, and do the job herself.*

That night, when all the household was asleep, Malvina went down to the cellar to cast a spell taught to her by her mother, a powerful *bruja*. As a sliver of moonlight cut through the small window, Malo combined secret oils and called upon the forces of hell. She gathered the white feather of a chicken, an old piece of leather, a spindly, bent stick, and a cat's ragged toenail. Saying words too horrible to repeat, she drank the mixture.

In a few awful moments, she had turned into an old woman with hair as white as a chicken's feather, a body as thin and bent as a stick, and skin as rough as leather.

"*Bueno, bueno.* A perfect disguise." Her voice was as scratchy as a cat's paw. From her loose dress, Malvina pulled out an avocado, green and ripe.

From another pocket, she took out a bottle of oil. Its contents smelled of a tomb, and Malvina rubbed drops of the oil on the avocado.

"This will be the last thing that Blanca tastes." Her laugh was so frightening, it scared some nearby coyotes, who howled in reply.

And so, Malvina left the hacienda, headed for the Rancho García.

• • •

At the ranch, Blanca did not go with the brothers on their usual roundup. It was Paco's birthday. She was going to try her hand at cooking a special dinner that night.

Earlier that morning, the brothers had kissed her cheek as they left.

"Don't open the door to strangers," Toro said, scratching the ground with his boot to emphasize his point.

"I won't," she replied.

The day passed quickly as Blanca cleaned the house for the party and prepared food. But her thoughts occasionally wandered—to Oscar and how she secretly wished she could somehow see him again. For in their brief meeting, she had lost her heart to him, and only he could return it to her.

A soft knock on the door interrupted her thoughts.

"Oscar," she whispered hopefully.

"Is anyone home?" a strange voice called.

Blanca was about to open the door but stopped, worried that Malvina might have sent someone else to kill her. She peeked out the window. But it was a bent woman, as old as the land.

"*¡Pobrecita!*" Blanca opened the door.

"*¡Ay!*" Malvina said, rubbing her back. "I am a midwife and was robbed on my way to a church festival. Can you give me water?"

Blanca fetched water, and the old woman drank.

"When the brothers García come home, they can help you on your way," Blanca said. "You must stay and eat with us."

"You are so kind, little one. I wish I had something to repay you for your kindness. But wait . . ." Malvina held out the large avocado.

"I can't take it. You can eat it later," Blanca said.

Malvina wiped her eyes with her sleeve. "Please, take my present. *Por favor.*" Malvina took a knife and cut into the avocado.

Blanca didn't want to hurt the woman's feelings. "Thank you. Will you have some also?"

Malvina shook her head. "It's just for you."

Blanca nodded and ate a slice of avocado; she smiled at its taste and then fell to the floor, dead.

Laughing, laughing, Malvina nudged Blanca with her foot, enjoying her victory. "Now I am rid of this nuisance forever."

Then, the sound of horses.

Malvina saw the brothers coming through the gate and ran in the other direction, where her own horse waited. She leaped onto its back and galloped away.

"Oh, no!" cried the brothers all at once, seeing Blanca on the ground.

43

Paco leaned his head above her heart. *"Muerta, muerta."* He spotted the avocado near Blanca. "She has been poisoned."

Caballo wailed in pain, picked up the tainted fruit, and threw it in the fireplace.

Lazo saw Malvina riding away. *"¡Allá está!* That crone must be to blame. Come, Toro. Come, Plateado."

They rode their horses fast after Malvina, who was still disguised as an old hag.

"Stupid little men," Malvina called after them.

The evil woman's horse moved quickly, as if driven by the devil, but the *vaqueritos* were gaining on her. Because she was not familiar with the land, Malvina rode her horse straight toward a wide and wild river. Her horse stopped suddenly on the steep bank, throwing Malvina into the deep, rushing water. She thrashed about, trying to stay afloat. She screamed and sank below the surface.

The brothers rode up and watched helplessly as the woman disappeared down the river. They could not save her.

The three brothers returned home, where Blanca had been laid out on a bed.

"The woman who did this to our Blanca is also dead," Lazo told the other brothers. "The grave of water is what she deserved for such a horrible deed."

In their grief, they did not hear Oscar ride up outside. The young man had been searching for Blanca, hoping to win her as his wife. He walked inside the house and saw her lying silent, but still lovely.

"A wicked spell took her life," Cacto said, wiping away tears.

"I know a good and wise *curandera*," Oscar said. "I'll fetch her. I pray she can help."

Oscar mounted his horse and galloped to a village where he found the woman, named Isidra.

Isidra lit candles all around Blanca, then shooed the brothers and Oscar outside, because healers don't give away their secrets. For one full day and night, Isidra said prayers and boiled special herbs.

As the sun set into the purple light of evening, Isidra came out of the house and welcomed the brothers and Oscar.

"Enter. Kiss her and let her know your love," the woman advised Oscar. "You saw and believed that Blanca's beauty was not only on the outside but the inside as well."

Oscar took nervous steps toward Blanca and kissed her lightly. Her lips were as sweet as he imagined heaven. Before he could pull back, Blanca's pretty brown eyes were looking at him. She smiled.

"It's good to see you again," she said.

The brothers cheered with joy, and Oscar embraced her. They told her the story of what happened and about the fate of the old hag, who Blanca realized must have been Malvina in disguise. That night, they celebrated with a fiesta until the sun came up, bright with possibilities.

"It's time for me to go home," Blanca said to the brothers. "But I'll return every fall to help with the roundup."

She took Oscar's hand. "I would like you to meet my father. I know he'll love you as much as I do."

Blanca and Oscar started off to her *rancho*. Rain began to fall, but this time it was like shimmering drops of new love.

The river into which Malvina fell was renamed Río Malo. *Vaqueros* who pass during a storm claim they hear a woman screaming, and they quickly ride in the other direction.

El Día de los Muertos

THE WHITE PYRAMIDS rose into the sky of blue, bluer than the waters of the lake surrounding the splendid place of the eagle and the cactus—Tenochtitlán.

"Pay attention to your work, Nochehuatl," said the feather craftsman to his son.

"Yes, I am sorry, Father," Nochehuatl answered.

When his father wasn't watching, however, the young man continued to admire the great city of white stone and magnificent palaces. Nochehuatl had been born with a great love of life. He looked toward his future as though it were the ascent to a grand temple. He was working at a respected trade, the art of featherwork. His feather pieces sat on the heads of noblemen and adorned the shields and banners of brave warriors. Perhaps someday they would even decorate the body of the emperor. Nochehuatl believed this was his destiny, and with his constant, steadfast labor and study, he was becoming a true craftsman.

With dyes from blue clay, yellow ocher, red from the insects found nestled in cactus, and violet from mollusks, Nochehuatl created wondrous pictures of birds, butterflies, and serpents.

Nochehuatl's feather work sold fast whenever he and his father took their wares to the marketplace, which was set within sight of the great palace of the emperor.

Nochehuatl found the market exciting.

The scent of chilies and spices hung in the air like early morning fog over Lake Texcoco. On sale was the bounty of the earth: onions, maize, tomatoes, honey, sweet potatoes, and jicama. *Cacaoteros* sold cacao beans, which would be roasted and ground to make chocolate.

Furs of otter, badger, rabbit, and deer were spread out for all to see, so lush they seemed ready to spring back to life.

Nobles bedecked in royal turquoise, jade necklaces, and gold pendants strode by. Cacao beans, quills of gold, feathers, pieces of tin, and copper axes traded hands with each purchase, and not without a few words of hard bargaining.

Yet something more was in the breeze this day, a freshness and sense of expectation.

With agave thread, Nochehuatl was sewing together feathers from parrots and macaws when he looked up. There, gazing down at his display, was a lovely young woman. Her dark eyes held many secrets. Her hair was like a night of dreams.

"Do you want to buy something?" he asked.

She shook her head and smiled, and he felt as if his heart would lift his body off the ground.

"This is beautiful." Her voice was like the music from the clay flutes played at religious ceremonies. "I just wanted to admire your work."

Nochehuatl nodded in gratitude.

She began to walk away.

"Wait!" Nochehuatl shouted, and ran after her. "What is your name?"

"Xochiyotl."

"I am Nochehuatl. Thank you, Xochiyotl, for making this glorious day even more glorious."

She smiled again and walked on.

Nochehuatl watched her go and whispered her name over and over. It meant "heart of a gentle flower."

Every day afterward at the market he waited for Xochiyotl to pass by him, which she did on the way to taking food to her father, a potter. She would always stop to talk to Nochehuatl. They shared laughter, a reverence for life, a respect for the gods, and a strong connection with family.

Nochehuatl and Xochiyotl saw the good in each other and soon fell in love.

"Father, I want to marry Xochiyotl," Nochehuatl said one evening as they were packing up after the day at the market.

"Are you sure, my son?"

"Father, I would do anything for her."

The feather craftsman smiled. "Then I will see the matchmaker."

He did so, and the matchmaker, a large woman, visited Xochiyotl's father the next day. Nochehuatl could not concentrate on his featherwork until he knew whether Xochiyotl's father would agree to the match. His fingers felt awkward and slow as the day passed. At last, the matchmaker arrived at their house, a frown on her big face. Nochehuatl's heart sank to the bottom of the lake.

Then she grinned.

"She will have you, young Nochehuatl," the matchmaker said. "Now get me something to drink for my labors."

As Nochehuatl's love for Xochiyotl grew, so did his mastery of featherwork. His winged serpents appeared as if they would fly off shields. His feathered cloaks were like delicate human wings. His headdresses resembled feathery exotic flowers. Nobles came from the far reaches of the empire to buy them.

The day was set for their marriage. At morning's break, Nochehuatl's mother and female relatives ground maize to make tamales, mixing meat

53

with the corn dough and wrapping it in corn husks. Sweet *octli* was prepared for the elders.

In the evening, Nochehuatl saw the light of torches approaching their house. Xochiyotl was carried on the back of one of her kinswomen, who counseled her on marriage along the way. His beloved smiled, and he had never seen her so radiant. Red feathers were pasted on Xochiyotl's arms and legs, so that she looked like a mythical creature. Her face was painted with fine pyrite, which glittered like a sunset.

With incense burning, making the air thick and fragrant, Nochehuatl and Xochiyotl sat on a mat, and a fire was started in the hearth. His cape was knotted to her shift by the matchmaker.

Then Nochehuatl's mother fed Xochiyotl mouthfuls of tamale and more to her son.

Their marriage was complete.

"I will love you forever," Nochehuatl told his new wife in their bedchamber.

"Nothing will separate us," she replied.

They talked of family and of Nochehuatl's work, of his someday becoming a master feather craftsman.

Soon after, Xochiyotl found she was with child.

"You will have a son to carry on your work, my husband," she told him. Nochehuatl hugged her and thanked the gods for his good fortune.

54

But . . .

Happiness is sometimes as hard to hold on to as a cloud, even for good people.

One day, after returning from the market, Nochehuatl found Xochiyotl on the floor. Her eyes were closed. Her chest barely moved with life.

Nochehuatl ran to his mother's house. "Come quick—my wife is ill."

His mother hurried back with him. Nochehuatl paced outside, his artisan's hands wringing, wringing.

"Nochehuatl, my son." His mother's voice and sad eyes foretold the outcome he had feared. "Xochiyotl and the baby are gone."

He rushed into the room and took Xochiyotl's body in his arms. He held her for a full day until his father had to take her away for burial. "No," was all Nochehuatl could say as they carried her away, and he repeated it again and again, like the mournful chant of the priests.

For days, for weeks, Nochehuatl rarely slept or ate, and his eyes became stony. He had no interest in his work or in living without his Xochiyotl.

When he could no longer stand the misery, he lay prostrate on the floor of his workroom and prayed to the goddess Mictecacihuatl. That day marked the beginning of the feast of Miccailhuitontli, which was dedicated to her, and to the dead.

"O Lady of the Dead," he prayed, "please bring my Xochiyotl back to me."

Nochehuatl pleaded until he was weak. As he lay exhausted on the floor, he heard the goddess.

"Nochehuatl," said a whisper of a voice within his mind, like a thought.

He raised his head. No one was in the room with him.

"It is Mictecacihuatl, and I have come to answer your prayer," the whisper of a voice said.

Nochehuatl thanked the goddess.

"Go beyond the city to a cave and enter it," she said. "There, you will find Huitzilopochtli, the Sinister Hummingbird. Beyond the sun and moon, the war god had a sacred vision of an eagle devouring a snake wrapped around a cactus on an island in the middle of a lake. That prophecy was given to his priests, who passed it on for generations. After years of wandering, your people saw that eagle on an island. And there they built this city you call Tenochtitlán. Find the mighty Huitzilopochtli, and ask for the soul of your beloved. He is the keeper of many souls."

"I will go," Nochehuatl said.

As he paddled a canoe from the city of Tenochtitlán to the shores of the lake, he grew fearful. Huitzilopochtli was the fiercest of the gods. Still, Nochehuatl kept on, driven by love for his dead wife.

Holding a torch, Nochehuatl found the cave and entered. Down into the darkness he walked, until it seemed as if he had passed through another time. At last, he saw light ahead.

He breathed deeply.

A cavern was lit with hundreds of torches. On a throne of skulls sat Huitzilopochtli. He had the face of a handsome, strong warrior, for it is said he once was a man. But his eyes were like fiery sunsets. He wore a headdress made of hummingbirds that flitted their wings madly. He held a shield and darts, weapons of war.

Nochehuatl bowed low. "Mighty Huitzilopochtli, please return my Xochiyotl. You have many souls, and she is my life."

58   A dreadful silence.

Then Nochehuatl heard a rumble in the back of his head. It was the god speaking to him, within his mind, because Huitzilopochtli did not move his lips.

"Your prayers have moved me," the voice said. "You shall have your Xochiyotl."

From the darkness, she stepped forth, rubbing her eyes as if arising from sleep. When the lovers saw each other, day seemed to come into the cave.

"My love, my love," Nochehuatl murmured. They held each other for a long time.

"We will be together forever," she replied, tears in her eyes.

Nochehuatl bowed to the god. "Huitzilopochtli, we thank you. You are most generous." He took Xochiyotl's hand and they turned to leave.

"Wait," the war god rumbled.

Nochehuatl stopped and shivered.

"She may leave with you," Huitzilopochtli said, "but you must not look back at her to see if she is following. You must trust that I will keep my word. If you do not trust me and turn around, she must return to the dead."

"I shall not look back," Nochehuatl vowed.

And so he and Xochiyotl started the journey up and up from the heart of the earth. Nochehuatl's happiness supported him as they walked. Nearing the entrance, however, he began to worry that he had been tricked by Huitzilopochtli. Fear began to rot his bravery.

"Xochiyotl, are you there? My heart of a gentle flower, can you hear me?" he said.

No answer.

He asked again. He looked up and saw the sky's light ahead. But he could not risk losing Xochiyotl again. He turned around.

Briefly he saw her, a sad smile on her face and her mouth calling his name silently as she faded like nightfall back into the cave.

Nochehuatl wept. He returned to Tenochtitlán, as broken as pottery on a stone floor.

Refusing to work or eat, Nochehuatl soon became ill, and one year after his trip to the cave, again during the month of the Lady of the Dead, he joined his love in death.

And some say that when the moon is high over the great pyramids of Tenochtitlán, when the great market is silenced, then the figure of Nochehuatl appears on Lake Texcoco, paddling his small canoe to the cave to join his Xochiyotl.

Juan and the Pinto Bean Stalk

JUAN HITCHED UP HIS BAGGY PANTS and pulled down his bandanna so low that he could barely see. He did look fine, but he *didn't* look where he was going, and ran into his mother.

She clicked her tongue. "*Hijo*, get a job, we need food," she said, and pulled up his bandanna so she could see his big brown eyes.

"I'm too cool to work, Mom."

"You never take things seriously." She tapped his head gently with her finger. "You know your father died and left us poor, *hijo*, and my job at the laundry doesn't pay well. If we don't do something, we'll go hungry."

Juan barely listened, and his mother shook her head, wondering how she could have raised such a lazy boy.

"Oh, man," Juan said, pulling on his tennis shoe. He had heard these words before.

"Juan." His mother spoke firmly. "Take Old Vaca out and sell her so we can buy food for the table."

Her shoulders sagged pitifully. She pulled up a chair and looked into his eyes. "*Hijo*, I have golden dreams for you. I dream you will finish school and go to college and get a good job. I dream your children will never know hunger."

He knew his mother was right. Their house was as tiny as a jail cell and just as grim. She hardly smiled anymore, and Juan was tired of eating beans, eggs, and tortillas every day. He knew he wasn't helping as much as he should, but when the bros asked him to skip school, he couldn't resist, and they often ended up at the nearby beach, watching girls.

"Mom, school is hard, life is tough," he said. "It's easier just to hang on the corners and listen to music."

"Juan, I didn't finish school." His mother glanced around their little kitchen. "And this is all I could get without an education." She held out her cracked, red hands. "I want better for you. Now, go sell Old Vaca, and we will be able to eat for a few days more."

"Okay," Juan said, checking in a mirror to make sure he still looked good.

Old Vaca sat in the front yard. She was a white station wagon with black rust spots and holes in the upholstery. Her tires were bald, but luckily they weren't flat, and the radio still worked, though the car coughed and burped along. Juan turned up the sound and rolled out into the street. He slid low in the seat because he didn't want his friends to see him in such a piece of junk as Old Vaca.

As he turned one corner looking for a used car lot, a white light flashed in his eyes. He shut them, and when he opened them again, there was a junkyard that he hadn't noticed before with a sign that read WE BUY CARS.

"I've never seen this place," Juan said to himself. "It must be new."

He pulled in. Old Vaca sputtered to a stop, steam coming from the hood.

65

"Can I help you?" said a man who was three feet tall and didn't look a day over ninety-five years old. He wore all black, including dark sunglasses.

"I'd like to sell this car." Juan patted the roof of Old Vaca.

The old man kicked a tire, and Juan prayed it wouldn't blow.

"I like this car. It has a lot of history to it," the *viejito* wheezed. "I will give you something special for it."

"Like what?"

"This." The *viejito* held out his hand and opened it to show three dried pinto beans.

Juan laughed. "Are you trying to rip me off? That's not even enough to make one tostada."

The *viejito* laughed. "These are not ordinary beans. They are magic." The old man's eyes brightened. "Just plant them and stand back. They will make your dreams come true."

"How about giving me two hundred dollars instead?" Juan was determined to show his mother that he was a good businessman.

"You must consider the big picture, young man, what lies ahead. Look again." The beans glowed like stars in the night.

Juan blinked to make sure he wasn't seeing things. The beans seemed to hum a song. The *viejito* held them close to Juan's ears, and now they began to sing to him, or at least he thought it was a song. They said, *Magic beans are an easier way to get a big house and big car and big TV. No school. No getting a good job. No work. Only magic.*

"I'll take them," Juan told the old man.

"*Bueno, bueno.*" The *viejito* wheezed again. He put the beans in Juan's hand. "Remember, magic always needs a little help." But Juan didn't hear him; he was already running home.

At the corner, Juan turned back and noticed that the old junkyard had disappeared in another flash of light.

Juan picked up his pace until he was back home, a triumphant grin on his face.

His mother met him at the gate. "How much money did you get for Old Vaca? I bet it was a lot." She beamed.

Juan held out his hand and showed her the beans. "Mom, I traded in Old Vaca for these magic beans."

"What have you done? Please don't tell me that you sold our only car for those dried-up old pinto beans. Please say it is a joke!"

"It's no joke. The beans *are* magic. They will make our dreams come true without any sweat."

His mother snatched the beans from his hand and threw them in the yard, directly on the spot where Old Vaca had rested. "We'll surely starve now."

"But, Mom—"

"*¡Silencio!* Do your homework so you won't have to think about your stomach hurting from being so empty." She left for her job, slamming the door behind her. Juan waited and then went outside.

"Do your stuff, beans." Juan planted and watered the beans, then went into the house. He glanced out the window but saw no magic, just a patch of brown dirt. He did his homework and checked again. No magic. He watched and watched until he fell asleep.

The morning light danced on his eyelids, golden and fresh and warm. Juan stretched. He headed to the bathroom, but stopped when he saw something out of the corner of his eye.

He whistled.

In the yard was a pinto bean stalk at least four feet thick and headed straight to the sky. Juan rushed outside. He fell over backward trying to see the top of the green plant, because it reached past the clouds. He touched the bean stalk to make sure he wasn't dreaming. But no, up there were his dreams, just for the taking.

Juan picked himself off the ground and ran inside, dressing quickly. He would let his mother sleep. He began to climb the branches of the pinto bean stalk.

"This is like climbing green, round money," he said, laughing to himself.

Two hours later, he was still climbing. But he no longer smiled. The bean stalk smelled of *frijoles*, and he remembered he hadn't eaten since the night before.

"This ain't so easy," Juan muttered to himself. "Maybe it takes work, just like Mom said."

Far above his neighborhood, far above the city, the sky was never so blue and the clouds never so white.

He climbed on until his legs and arms ached.

Bump.

"Ow." He rubbed his head.

He had hit a slab of brown earth, so large he couldn't see where it ended or began. Juan pulled himself up through a hole and stood tall. "I climbed this all myself."

He looked around at this world at the top of the pinto bean stalk.

"Holy *pozole!*" The trees were taller than skyscrapers. In fact, they looked as if they tickled the sky and made it laugh blue.

Suddenly a glint of metal shone in the distance. "That must be where the treasure is," Juan said confidently.

Then he sighed. This was not going to be like a walk to the 7-Eleven for a microwave burrito and a soda. This was going to be a journey. Juan started off with determination. His pants kept trying to slide down, and he wished they weren't so baggy.

On he walked until he recognized that the glint was a tall building, silver and shiny with gold trim. It had one large door and no windows.

"How will I get in?" Juan scratched his head.

At that moment, the door opened with a squeak and out stepped a giant woman, a woman as big as an apartment building. She wore a white apron that could have covered a lake. Her two braids were like long ropes of midnight.

She threw water from a bucket. Juan ran but got splashed and soaked anyway. He sputtered and coughed.

"Who's there?" the woman asked.

Juan stumbled out from the grass where he was hiding. He sneezed.

"Poor boy," the *giganta* said. Then she picked Juan up and put him in her pocket.

He was in darkness, and whenever the large woman walked, he bounced like a coin on a trampoline. When the *giganta* pulled him out of her pocket at last, he was on a wooden table the size of a football field.

"Here is some *pan*, little man. Eat, eat," she said, her voice very tiny for one so huge.

The bread was as tall as Juan, but he ate until his stomach became as round and hard as a bowling ball.

Giganta sat in a chair and pulled a pipe out of her other pocket. "This is the home of El Grande, the giant of this land. *El jefe*. He's rich as a king because he steals from everyone, and he loves to eat people for breakfast, more people for lunch, and then take a siesta and eat yet more people for dinner."

Juan shivered.

"And just because El Grande is bigger than anyone else, he thinks that everything is easy and for the taking. He doesn't have to work hard like the rest of us," she said.

Juan bowed his head as if Giganta was talking about *him*. He also yawned, sleepy from his full stomach and the long trip up the bean stalk.

"I made you a bed inside this matchbox." The *giganta* picked Juan up and placed him in the box, where she had put a piece of cloth just the right

size for him. She put the matchbox on a top shelf. "*Buenas noches*, little man."

Juan slept, but dreamed that the earth was shaking and he was falling down the bean stalk. He woke up and realized that the rumble was not a dream. The walls of the house rattled as if an earthquake had struck.

"El Grande is coming," the *giganta* warned him. "Hide, hide."

Behind the sugar jar, Juan shook with fright.

The door banged open and in walked El Grande.

El Grande's teeth were as tall as streetlights and as yellow as bananas, and there was enough hair in his mustache to make wigs for all the bald men in the world.

"*Mujer*, bring me my *café*," El Grande boomed.

Juan held his nose. El Grande's breath smelled of trash cans, dead cats, and burps.

Giganta brought the giant a steaming cup the size of a swimming pool.

"*Mujer*, bring me my *cena*!" El Grande yelled.

Giganta served the giant on plates the size of space ships. "We were all out of people for you to eat, El Grande. Instead, I have cooked sixteen cows and twenty-five turkeys."

"*Mujer*, bring me my *pollo*!" El Grande yelled after the dinner, which he ate in one disgusting, greedy gulp.

"My mom would yell at me if I ate that fast," Juan whispered to himself in his spot behind the sugar jar.

74

Giganta brought a scrawny chicken to the giant.

El Grande smiled, but it was a wicked smile. "Lay for me."

The chicken stretched its neck. "No."

"What!" El Grande bellowed so loud that Juan was almost blown off the shelf.

"I said, Lay, *pollo*," El Grande boomed again. "Give me a *huevo*."

The hen strutted and squawked and out popped an egg, gold and round.

"*Bueno*," El Grande said. "Now I am tired. I had a hard day of eating people and stealing riches."

He rose and stretched. Then his great nose sniffed the air.

"*AY YI YI YO*, I SMELL THE BLOOD OF A LAZY *NIÑO*."

Juan began to say his prayers.

"You're smelling the people you ate last night. Now, go to bed," Giganta said. "You need rest if you are going out tomorrow to steal more money and terrorize more people."

El Grande sniffed again, this time unsure of himself. "I'm going to sleep." He stomped out of the room.

Giganta pushed aside the sugar jar. "Good night, boy. Keep out of sight or you will be El Grande's next snack."

"*Buenas noches y gracias*." Juan suddenly ran over and kissed her large cheek.

Giganta smiled and went to her bedroom. Soon the house rumbled

75

with snores from El Grande and the big woman. Even the *pollo* snoozed in her basket.

Juan knew what he must do. He shinned down the shelf, stopping occasionally to pick slivers from his legs, and then climbed up the table. He held the chicken's beak shut.

"Shut up or I'll make chimichangas out of you."

The *pollo* screeched. Juan feared he would be crushed because the chicken was the size of a horse.

Juan thought about the giant in the other room and felt bad for talking so mean to the chicken. "I'm sorry. Please come with me, *pollo*. My mom and me are poor and we need you. I promise to treat you good and not cook you when you don't lay any golden *huevos*."

The *pollo* cackled with pleasure. It was the first time anyone had ever said "please" to her.

"Let's go. I could use a change of scenery," the chicken clucked.

"Great." Juan whooped. Then he put his hands over his mouth.

"*AY YI YI YO, I DO SMELL THE BLOOD OF A LAZY NIÑO!*" roared El Grande from the other room.

"Let's get out of here," Juan and the *pollo* said at the same time.

Juan scrambled down the leg of the table, while the *pollo* fluttered down, and both sped out of the room just as El Grande came into the kitchen.

"I will eat me a boy and a chicken," the giant yelled.

Juan had never run so fast. As he ran, he promised God that he would finish school and go to college and get a good job if he could only see his mother again. El Grande got closer. The *pollo* squeaked with fright and kept laying gold eggs, which Juan stopped and picked up until his pockets bulged.

"*Venga, mi hijo,*" shouted El Grande in a fatherly voice. "I won't hurt you. I will adopt you and you will inherit all I have."

"Do you believe him?" Juan asked the chicken.

"No. If you stop, we'll both be squashed flatter than a quesadilla," the *pollo* replied.

Juan picked up the pace.

Then Juan came to the hole where the pinto bean stalk grew. With the *pollo* behind him, Juan slid down, ignoring the bumps. Through the clouds he went, until he saw the haze of the city sky and smelled the cars' exhaust and knew he was near home.

Above, he saw El Grande following.

Slam.

Juan hit bottom. He led the *pollo* into the house to recover and raced back into the yard, where he found a rusted saw.

Back and forth, Juan sawed at the pinto bean stalk.

"I'm so sorry I didn't listen to Mom and clean this saw," he said to himself, not even halting to wipe the sweat from his brow. All the while, El Grande grew closer.

Crack.

The pinto bean stalk started to fall. El Grande looked down and realized his situation.

77

"OH, NO!" The giant yelled so loud that it shattered every window in the barrio.

El Grande and the pinto bean stalk dropped into the ocean. The splash caused rain for a week and a half afterward, but the horrible giant was never heard from again.

"Juanillo, Juanillo," his mother shouted, seeing her son with a saw in one hand and the stump of the pinto bean stalk behind him, "are you all right?"

"*Sí*, Mom." Juan hugged his mother and thanked God for getting him home safe. "We will never be poor again."

He dug into his pockets and pulled out gold eggs. "You were right, Mom. Nothing in life is easy. I found that dreams are not up a pinto bean stalk or in the sky, but in hard work."

79

"That, my son, is the most valuable of lessons—more valuable than golden eggs."

Keeping his promise, Juan went to school, did his homework, and got a good job, so that even without the golden eggs, he could take care of his mother very well.

Sometimes, he walked to the edge of the ocean where El Grande had fallen, and on quiet days he could have sworn that the tide carried the words "*AY YI YI YO*, I STILL SMELL THE BLOOD OF A LAZY *NIÑO*."

The Piper of Harmonía

Every town has a memory.

I am the memory of Harmonía. I am the teller of stories and the keeper of the recollections. Of course, not all of them are happy. Like the story of Harmonía itself . . .

HARMONÍA WAS A BEAUTIFUL TOWN. At its back were the blue-green Sangre de Cristo Mountains. All around were fields of black earth, where farmers grew plenty of wheat, pumpkins, and corn. On pastures of thick, sweet grass, sheep and cows became fat.

The town was alive with children. Their laughter and shouting rang throughout the streets. Mostly they played in the large Plaza de las Flores in the center of town. The pink stones of the plaza and its fountain were surrounded by flowers, making the air smell like a bride's bouquet. The children played card games. They hooted when they won and sighed when they lost. They teased and sang. They skipped and ran. They chased after each other, told stories, and splashed in the fountain water, leaving small wet footprints on the pink stones.

The children were healthy and full of joy, even Tomás, whose right leg had been injured. He used a wooden crutch and could not run. His mother had died when he was a baby; he was being raised by his father, Ricardo the baker. Although he had plenty to be bitter about, Tomás was loving and generous, and well liked by the other children. His best friend was Hito, the son of Mayor Fernando. Hito always waited for Tomás to catch up when they walked. In the summer, they played dominoes for hours on the grass near the plaza.

82   One day, as was his custom, Mayor Fernando was walking around the town, arms behind his back, proud of what he saw.

Hito ran up to him.

"Papá, come and play with me and Tomás in the plaza." Hito tugged on his father's coattails.

"I am too busy now, son. I have a whole town to look after."

Disappointed, Hito went back to the plaza. His father rarely played with him, but Hito never stopped hoping that he would someday.

The mayor resumed his walk but didn't get far before he heard a commotion in the plaza. He went to see what was disturbing another perfect day in Harmonía.

Children screamed and scampered about because the stones of the plaza were covered with lizards. The lizards were the size of a man's hand and had long pointed claws. They were as green as deceit, and marked with black spots. Their tongues whipped in and out, tasting the air.

"Men, grab shovels, axes, and sticks," the mayor yelled. *"¡Rápido!"*

They did as the mayor asked, and attacked the lizards, but the animals were much too fast. They sped off into bushes before the men could even touch them. Even old Father Molina joined in the chase, although he often had to stop and pick off the lizards that crawled up his cassock.

Meanwhile, the women gathered up the younger children, while the lizards nipped at their ankles. The older children ran out of the plaza, all except for Tomás and Hito. With his crutch, Tomás tried to shoo the little creatures away, but they snapped at him and his friend.

Just then, Tomás's father, Ricardo, arrived, having heard all the noise. Ricardo scooped up his son in one arm and Hito in the other, and ran back to the safety of his bakery.

"What's happening, Papá?" Tomás said.

"I don't know. But you and Hito stay here." Ricardo went to help the other men.

The battle lasted until dark. At midnight, the lizards just seemed to leave. Many had been killed, and men shoveled up the bodies, placing them in a wagon so they could be buried outside of town.

Exhausted, the men leaned on their shovels.

"Señor Mayor, what do you make of this?" said Luís, who ran the café.

"Maybe evil has come to our town," Father Molina suggested.

The men made quick signs of the cross, just in case.

83

But the mayor already had an explanation, as he always did. After all, he was a man of Science, Progress, and Money. "It just got too dry in the desert, so the lizards headed to a place with plenty of water," he said. "This was all an accident of nature."

"Yes, that's what it was," Luís agreed.

By that time, Tomás and Hito had rejoined the adults.

"Will they return, Papá?" Tomás asked Ricardo.

"I hope not, my son."

However, Hito was still frightened, and stood close to his father.

The other men decided that the mayor was right. They would never see the lizards again.

And they didn't—until the next day, when even more lizards descended on Harmonía. This time, they invaded the houses, entering through the smallest cracks. The women swept them out with brooms and placed rags under the doors. The town was filled with shrieks as people found lizards under beds and in beds, on tables and in cupboards, in their pockets and in their shoes.

Women yelled as they chased them away from babies' cribs. The lizards scurried over red-tiled roofs and dropped onto the heads of whoever passed by. People stepped carefully when they went into their outhouses.

Lizards even climbed the adobe walls of the Church of the Blessed Mother, near the plaza. Father Molina said a rosary as he tried to scare them off with a rake.

Like a green army, lizards slithered down streets, bellies low to the dirt, eyes straight ahead. The daily *mercado* had to be closed because they climbed over the fruit and vegetables, and bit the fingers of the merchants.

Everyone was scared—except the children. Once they got used to the creatures, they played with them. They chased the lizards, then the lizards chased them.

"Let's try to catch a lizard, Tomás," Hito suggested. "We can try to tame him."

"They are too fast for me," Tomás said.

Hito stayed with his friend and watched as the other boys ran after a particularly big lizard.

Tomás and Hito walked to the plaza, where men gathered with torches.

The mayor shouted his new orders: "Chase them away with fire!"

The men spread out. The lizards did leave by nightfall. Unfortunately, the hotel had been accidentally burned down.

That night, the townspeople of Harmonía went to bed, tired from fighting lizards. They prayed that the scaly pests would move on to another town or return permanently to the desert.

The next morning all seemed quiet.

Ricardo woke early, as he always did to start his day of baking. He checked Tomás to make sure he was safe, and went to the kitchen. He looked out the window with relief. A calm morning and not one lizard.

Then, Ricardo went to pump some water. Out of the spigot came a stream of tiny lizards.

Ricardo woke up the mayor, who woke up other men. They walked the path to the mountain spring from which Harmonía's water came, and found it teeming with lizards.

As they tried futilely to shoo the lizards from the water, more bad news came from Farmer Joaquín, who had found the group of men at the spring.

"The lizards are in our grain," he panted.

The men ran to the grain house. Inside were lizards so round from eating that they waddled, which at least made them easy to kill.

Then Rancher Miguel arrived. "The lizards are scaring my livestock. My cows and sheep have busted through the fences."

"We must have a town meeting!" the mayor announced.

The church bell rang, and everyone gathered in the town hall. The place was full of children playing; they had also tired of the lizards outside.

As the people entered for the meeting, the children had to stop playing and sit at the back on the floor. Tomás waved to Raymundo, the son of the tailor.

"I hope this meeting ends soon," Raymundo said. "I want to get back to my game of cards."

"Shhhh," an old woman said. "The mayor is ready to start."

The mayor sat at a large table at the front and tried to calm everyone. He shuffled his feet as a lizard ran across them.

"Please, my townspeople!" He had to speak loudly.

"God help us!" a woman shouted.

"We must leave this cursed town!" a man yelled.

Tomás sat at the back, holding on to his father's hand. He and the other children were the first to hear the music. But it was as if the notes called his name alone: *Tomás, Tomás, Tomás.*

He turned and saw a stranger standing in the doorway. He was tall and had a black mustache that hung down both sides of his mouth. He was dressed like a mariachi. His bright red pants and short yellow jacket were decorated with intricate purple braiding. His shirt was orange silk. Around his neck was tied a blue scarf. On his head was a white sombrero. His boots were as shiny black as a lizard's eyes. He winked at Tomás as he played a golden *flauta*. Although the music was soft, one by one people began to shut up and listen, and soon the only sound in the place was the mariachi's melody. The townspeople of Harmonía all turned to the stranger.

"I will help you," he said once he had their attention. His voice was as pure as his piping.

The mayor cleared his throat. "Who are you, *señor*?"

"Just call me Gaitero."

"*Mucho gusto.* But as you can see, Señor Gaitero, we are busy here," the mayor said. "We don't need music."

"Oh, yes, you do, Señor Mayor. With my music I can rid the town of these troublesome lizards. I cleared out a plague of mice from the town of Tanto, and I took away a curse of scorpions from the city of Caliente. Pay me five hundred golden coins and the lizards will be gone."

He left, playing an odd song on his flute.

"That man is loco," the mayor said. "Now, where were we?"

"Maybe we should pay," interrupted Esteban the cook.

"That is not necessary. I have a plan," the mayor said. "I will ask the farmers to bring in a wagon of poisoned grain and place it in piles around the plaza. The lizards will eat it and die."

The townspeople cheered. The children also cheered because the meeting was over and they could play again.

The next morning, the lizards swarmed into town in even greater numbers. Everywhere, people had to step around them or else get bitten on the toes.

In horse-drawn wagons, the farmers brought in the grain. The townspeople watched and waited.

The lizards ignored the grain.

"Now what shall we do?" Father Molina said.

At another town meeting, the people demanded that the piper be summoned.

"The lizards are eating our food and spoiling our water," said Ernesto, who made leather goods. "We have too much money invested in this town to leave it to lizards."

"No, I beg you. This piper shall bring nothing but trouble," Father Molina warned.

The people refused to listen.

"We want the piper!" they shouted.

And as they did, Gaitero appeared at the back of the town hall.

"I shall get rid of the lizards early tomorrow morning. Have my money ready by tomorrow night."

"*Gracias*, Señor Gaitero!" the people shouted, and clapped.

That night, Tomás did not sleep well and woke early. He dressed and walked out in the dim daylight. Then he heard the piper's music. The birds chirped along to the tune, which seemed to say, *Follow me, follow me, follow me.*

Tomás walked toward the tune, which came from the edge of town. In the distance, he saw the piper dancing as the music became a cyclone of melody. Soon the lizards appeared, picking up their tiny legs as if marching to the beat. There were so many that they resembled a giant green snake moving down the road.

The piper danced on and led them to a deep chasm at the foot of the mountains.

By the hundreds, the lizards jumped into the chasm. Tomás watched the creatures hurl themselves to their deaths.

When Ricardo awoke and didn't find Tomás in his bed, he became worried. He followed the lizards, and found his son.

"Papá, the piper is killing the lizards."

"It is good to see them go, but why do I still feel frightened?" Ricardo took his son's hand.

As he had promised, the piper had rid Harmonía of the lizards.

"Tell the mayor I will collect my money at midnight," the piper said to Ricardo, and went into the woods, playing the flute and dancing.

Ricardo spread the news. The mayor called for a fiesta that night. Happiness was in the air like the sound of the church bells. The children again ran around the plaza. Their laughter made music. They swatted at piñatas hanging from the limbs of trees and scrambled for the sweets and small toys that spilled out when one split open.

Hito grabbed handfuls for Tomás and himself.

"I kind of miss those old lizards," Hito said. "They were fun to play with."

"I don't. But I miss the piper's music," Tomás said. The Ramirez brothers played their guitars at the fiesta, but their music didn't call to him as the piper's songs had.

Still, the townspeople danced and the tables overflowed with corn, tortillas, rice, beans, and *carnitas*.

Their stomachs full, the people began to make excuses for why they shouldn't pay Gaitero.

"I think *he* was the one who brought the lizards, so we would pay him to get rid of them," said Amado the shoemaker.

His wife, Florinda, nodded. "That piper wants too much money. The mayor should have offered him less."

"Mamá, Papá, I'm getting tired," their daughter, María, whimpered.

"Go play. Can't you see the grown people are talking?" Amado shooed her away to the other children.

Antonio the butcher said, "I didn't trust that piper the moment I saw him."

"How do we really know that he led the lizards away? How do we know they didn't just leave?" added Pablo the blacksmith.

Ricardo stepped in. "Tomás and I saw the piper kill them. We can't go back on our word. We must pay him."

Candelario the merchant put down his plate of food. "Mayor, I demand you give the piper only half."

"Yes! Yes!" the people chimed in.

Tomás tugged on his father's pants. "Papá, won't Gaitero get angry if they don't give him all his money?"

His father nodded.

The mayor decided to follow the wishes of his people and give the piper only half the money. *The town needs the rest of it to repair the damage done by the lizards,* he thought.

At midnight, the piper appeared from the shadows. He was met in the street by the mayor and many townspeople, including Ricardo and Tomás.

The mayor cleared his throat. "Señor Gaitero," he said in his most authoritative voice, "we can give you only half of the money." Then he lied: "We can't raise the rest."

"What! *¡Dame mi dinero!*" The piper's voice lowered like a coming storm.

Tomás hid behind his father.

"Please, Mayor, I beg of you to pay this man," Ricardo said. "He saved Harmonía."

"Listen to him," the piper said. "You will lose if you play this game with me."

"You will take half or nothing at all," the mayor replied, glancing at his pocket watch and wanting to get to bed.

"Then I shall take nothing," the piper said calmly, and he walked back into the shadows, piping shrill music in his wake. To Tomás the eerie tune said, *They'll be sorry, they'll be sorry, they'll be sorry.*

The next day, Harmonía returned to normal.

Businesses opened their doors wide. People came to the market. Crops were ripe; cattle were ready for milking, sheep for shearing.

"Whatever became of the piper?" people wondered out loud, but most didn't think about it too long because there were more important things to do.

One morning, before the sun could warm the day, Tomás was awakened by the piper's music. *Come with me, come with me, come with me,* it seemed to call.

Tomás got out of bed and dressed. He heard the other children run past his house, skipping, laughing, jumping. His father did not stir. Tomás wanted to wake him, but the music pulled at him. *Come to a place where you can play forever. Come with me.*

He went outside. The rest of the children were well ahead of him. Hito ran past and waved.

"Do you hear? We are going to play. Play forever!" Hito sang out.

With his crutch, Tomás did his best to catch up, but still remained far behind.

"Wait for me," he called to Hito.

But Hito did not wait. He and the other children continued up the road to the mountains. Tomás could see them ahead, dancing to the piper's music.

The piper stopped in front of the granite wall of the mountainside. He played one long note and stopped. Silence. Then the mountain rumbled and yawned, and a large fissure opened. From the opening came a wonderful light, and in went all the children, holding hands and laughing.

"Wait!" Tomás called. But as he drew near, the crack began to close in front of him.

He did not reach it in time.

It was there that Ricardo found his son.

"*Mi hijo, mi hijo.*" He held Tomás tightly to him.

The boy told his father what had happened. "I was left behind. I won't be able to play forever with the other children," he said sadly.

"No, my son, but you will be able to grow into a man and have children of your own someday to watch over and love."

At first, none of the townspeople believed Tomás's story about the piper.

"Look at the footprints," Ricardo said. "They lead to the mountain, then disappear."

Mothers and fathers still searched for weeks, finding not one child.

"Do something!" the people demanded of the mayor at a meeting.

The mayor sent men to all corners of the county to look for the piper and bring him back so he could open the mountain, but Gaitero could not be found.

After that, the church was filled every day with people praying for their children to come back and asking for forgiveness.

But Harmonía had lost its blessings. The plaza was as quiet as a winter day. Crops failed; livestock became sick with fever. People moved away. The town died.

And that is my story. My name is Tomás. I am grown, with children of my own. I am the memory of Harmonía. The teller of stories. I tell the story of Gaitero over and over so that people will remember. I often visit Harmonía, which is now a ghost town, and there I pray that the piper will one day return and bring back the children—and hope—to the town.

Alejandro and the Spirit of the Magic Lámpara

FOR MILES AND MILES, nothing but rows and rows of green.

Alejandro wiped his brow and tugged at another weed choking a sugar beet. A few feet in front of him was his mother, and behind him, his father. His mother looked up and smiled.

How many summers had his family labored in the fields? How many summers had he wished he could go swimming and play ball like other kids? But Alejandro, who was nearing manhood, knew he had to work to support his family. So he pulled weeds one season, and the next season he moved irrigation pipe around the crops. He harvested strawberries and topped onions, and all without complaint.

But Alejandro always watched for magic in his hard life. He picked a broad green leaf off the sugar beet plant and held it up toward the sun, imagining it to be a wing from a mysterious bird. Alejandro held his breath, as if waiting for the whole field to take flight. Then he laughed and picked another weed.

At night, his family returned to their rundown shack in the nearby camp.

After helping to feed his five brothers and sisters and put them to bed, Alejandro walked beyond the lights of the camp and sat on the ground, counting stars, fancying each silver dot a fantastic kingdom of diamonds. Shooting stars summoned him to follow, though he knew not where.

And so the days passed.

One day, a stranger joined the crew in the field. He called himself Rico.

Rico's hair was peppery white. He was tall and thin, and all the other workers liked him immediately because he talked with friendliness and respect. But Alejandro saw that Rico's eyes had no light in them and that his mouth was set in an automatic smile, with no feeling behind it.

Alejandro said to his father, "Did you notice, Papi, that Rico's hands are smooth, like he hasn't worked hard a day in his life?" They were loading wood to bring in for the stove. "Did you also notice that Rico's back is straight and not bent from picking crops?"

"Rico said that he used to be a businessman," Alejandro's father replied, "but lost his money to a crook, so he was forced to find work in the fields. Poor man." His father picked up an armload of wood and shook his head at

Rico's misfortune. However, Alejandro's insides ached whenever he saw Rico, just like the time he had eaten too many strawberries.

After supper, Alejandro set off on one of his long walks. His mother disapproved because she said he needed his rest for the next day. But his father said, "Let the boy go," just before he fell asleep.

With the wide moon over his shoulder, Alejandro strolled for what seemed like miles. He loved the freedom and wondered, with a little guilt, what it would be like to work and live in the city. Most of all, he wanted to go to college, so he could become a doctor and care for poor people like his family. But that road seemed so far away, as far away as the stars he counted each night.

"It's a beautiful night, ¿verdad?"

Alejandro jumped. Behind him was Rico.

"I know what you wish for," Rico said. "I know you want to help your family. Well, I can help you."

"How?" Alejandro narrowed his eyes.

In the moonlight, Rico's face appeared even more deathly, although his voice shook with excitement. "I know a mine near here where there's a fortune, riches that you'll never see again in a lifetime, wealth that will solve your troubles and make your wishes come true."

"Why do you come to me?"

"I need a young pair of arms and legs to help me get it." Rico patted his hip. "My bones are brittle as a stick."

Alejandro bit his lip. Riches could buy a house for his family so they wouldn't have to travel from town to town, crop to crop, every year. And he could become a doctor. Alejandro asked Rico how far it was to the mine.

Rico pointed to a mountain at the edge of the fields that looked like a giant at rest. "Come with me."

"I better tell my family."

"No, no. I already told them and they gave their permission. I've borrowed a truck to get us there."

The mountain blocked out more and more of the stars as they neared it. Rico's teeth clattered with anticipation like maracas.

The old man hit the brakes. "We're here." He hopped out and ran to a hole cut in the mountain's side. "Down there is the fortune."

Rico's voice grew thinner but more eager. It made Alejandro feel a chill in the middle of the summer night.

Rico tied one end of a rope to a wooden beam and dropped the other end down the hole. He handed Alejandro a flashlight and pointed into the darkness.

"You may keep all the treasure you can carry. All I want is the old *lámpara* in the cave," Rico said.

Alejandro grew more suspicious. "That's all you want—an old *lámpara*? Why?"

"Do not ask questions. Just do as you're told, and you shall have a fortune." Rico's greed was as thick as the mud alongside an irrigation ditch.

Alejandro said a prayer to the Virgin Mary, then held his breath, grabbed the rope, and slid down into the hole. When his feet finally touched earth, he was able to breathe again.

Turning on the flashlight, Alejandro shielded his eyes, not because of the beam in all that darkness, but from all the gold. Golden masks of an ancient civilization were decorated with glittering gems. Coins of Spanish conquistadors burst from tattered bags. Precious necklaces and earrings tumbled out of shattered wooden boxes.

"I could never have imagined all this," Alejandro said to himself, the echo spinning around the cave. The gold was not yellow like the sun or the full moon, but deeper, shinier, and somehow a little sad.

As beautiful as the riches were, Alejandro was a bit afraid to touch the coins and jewelry, fearing they had been cursed by whoever left them behind.

"Never mind that *basura*," Rico yelled. "Look farther. Look for the *lámpara* on an altar stone."

Taking a few steps, Alejandro spotted a clay pot, cracked and dirty, with a string for a wick and a smell of old oil. He picked it up and shook his head. "Why does Rico want this old thing?" he wondered.

"Bring me the *lámpara*!" Rico's shout shook the cave.

"Okay, okay," Alejandro replied.

Alejandro began to climb the rope. Near the top, Rico reached out his arms. "Throw me the *lámpara*."

"No," replied Alejandro. "Get me out of here first."

"Give me the *lámpara*."

"No, I don't trust you."

Rico screamed with rage—a sound so sinister that it swirled around Alejandro like a whirlwind.

"Why won't you help me?" the young man said.

"You stupid boy! You were only useful to get that lamp! But if you won't give it to me, I will leave you to die. Then I will find another fool to help me. I'll return when you're nothing but bones."

"What about my family?" Alejandro said. "They need me."

"No, you need to die." Rico drew out a knife and cut the rope.

Down fell Alejandro, back into the blackness of the hole.

When he awoke, Alejandro rubbed his head. He cursed himself for being greedy like Rico and leaving his family alone.

"Wait," he said to himself. "I'm not dead yet. I'll find my way out of here."

Reaching into the darkness, he felt around for the flashlight, but it had broken into pieces. Alejandro sighed, then remembered the old *lámpara* in his shirt. He pulled it out and found a match in his pocket.

"Let's make you glow again," Alejandro said, and rubbed the pot with his shirt. Then he lit the wick.

Suddenly, the cave sparked with fireworks and filled with smoke that smelled as sweet as mystery and as ancient as history. Alejandro fell to the floor, covering his head with his hands. When the smoke cleared, he looked up. Before him was a giant serpent with red scales like the armor of warriors, purple eyes, wide and wise, and gigantic wings with feathers of green and blue like the jewels in the cave.

"Magic," Alejandro whispered.

He had waited for this moment his entire life, a moment when the world was transformed into a place with bewitching opportunities. But now that he was faced with it, he wished he was back in his bed.

"*¿Cómo está?*" the serpent thundered. The voice was ghostly.

Alejandro gulped.

The serpent gave a blast of laughter, enough to make Alejandro cover his head once more. "Do not be afraid. I am the soul of the *lámpara*, a spirit from ages ago."

"How'd you get in there?" Alejandro peeked inside the tiny opening.

"Good question. I was placed in the *lámpara* by the Spanish when they conquered the people who worshiped me. The Spaniards followed the Christian God. One minute I was on top of my temple; the next I was inside that stinky lamp. I owe you a debt for freeing me."

"It was my pleasure." Alejandro nodded. "It must have been terrible in there."

"Yes, it was, and it is so good to be out." The serpent stretched its wings. "Now I am at your service and will grant you three of your most secret desires."

"Really?"

"Those are the rules." The serpent extended its neck and tapped its pointy tail. "Well?"

Alejandro scratched his head, thinking, *First I want to get out of here, but I don't want to waste any wishes on it.*

The serpent's eyes became big and dreamy. "Once I have granted your wishes, I will no longer be a slave to whoever possesses the *lámpara*. Then I can join my fellow spirits. I long to see them, and I'm very sure none of them was trapped in an old *lámpara* like me."

108

Alejandro had an idea. "Serpent, you should see the outside world. There are flying machines and boxes that show colorful pictures."

The serpent yawned.

"And there are temples that reach up to the heavens. They're called sky-scrapers."

The serpent smiled.

Alejandro frowned. "Too bad we have to remain here until after I've made my wishes. I know once you see them, you can tell your friends the most wondrous stories."

"Hold on to my neck. I must see those scrapers of the sky."

Alejandro jumped on, and into the daylight they flew, over the mountain, soaring above farmland and highways. They cut through clouds to the city and the skyscrapers built of glass and steel.

"If we had had temples this big, those pesky Spaniards would not have banished me into the *lámpara*." The serpent hissed his regret.

Then he stopped, hovering with his large wings.

"Oh, no." The creature rocked its giant head, almost shaking Alejandro off to the streets below. "You tricked me. Just like the Spaniards. Maybe you don't deserve those wishes."

"Sorry, but remember the rules," Alejandro said. "Besides, what if I wish you back into the *lámpara*?"

"You do not look that cruel."

"I'm not," Alejandro said. "So please, let's land so I can think about my wishes."

The serpent flew back to the mountain, landing outside the cave, while Alejandro paced and contemplated what he wanted.

"Serpent," he said after a while, "I am ready for my first wish."

"*¿Sí?*" the serpent said.

Alejandro breathed deep. "I wish for enough money to buy my father and mother their own home and farm—enough so they won't have to follow the crops anymore, and enough to send me to school so I can become a doctor."

The serpent gave him a toothy grin. "You are not a greedy one. I like that."

Unfolding its wings, the serpent enclosed Alejandro. "When you are ready to make your other wishes, rub the *lámpara* and I shall come. Now shut your eyes and your first wish shall be true."

Alejandro shut his eyes. As soon as he opened them, he found himself at a beautiful home in a valley lush with crops. His father drove up in a nice truck and put his arm around his son. "I'm going to miss you, *hijo*, when you go to medical school."

Alejandro was stunned.

"Come inside—your mother is making enchiladas for your going-away party."

In the house, his mother sang as she cooked.

"Thank you, serpent," Alejandro whispered into the *lámpara*, which he noticed he was holding.

The years went quickly for Alejandro, who proved a good student. After many years of schooling, he returned home a doctor and opened a clinic for farmworkers. During that time, he had not thought of the *lámpara*, which was locked away in a closet in his office.

He loved being a doctor and healing the people who could not afford any other care. The clinic was so busy Alejandro had to hire another nurse. Her name was Bonita, and like her name she was pretty, but also tender-hearted.

They fell in love and married. Instead of counting stars, Alejandro counted the blessings of love, wife, and family—things no cave of gold could give him. He didn't tell Bonita about the magic serpent or the cave, nor why he kept the old *lámpara* locked in his office. He kept telling himself he should make more wishes and then set the spirit free, but he couldn't think of what else he wanted in life.

One day, when Alejandro was out of the clinic on business, an old man came in.

"My bones hurt," he told Bonita.

"Let me help, *señor*," Bonita said.

The old man whimpered, seemingly in pain. "I didn't have enough money to pay my bills, and my lights were turned off. So I fell in the dark."

"I'm sorry," Bonita said. "Wait. My husband has an old oil *lámpara* you can borrow. I'm sure he won't miss it."

"You're very kind," the visitor said.

Bonita did not know the old man was Rico.

As soon as she left the room for the lamp, Rico jumped up and danced around. *At last, it will be mine,* the old man sang to himself.

Bonita returned and held out the *lámpara* to him. "Here it is."

Rico grabbed it away from her. "You pretty fool."

The old man rubbed the *lámpara*, and the giant serpent appeared once more, rubbing its large purple eyes. "You forgot about me, didn't you? It always happens. One wish and people see nothing but gold."

The serpent took one look at Rico. "Who are *you*?"

"Your master."

"You sound greedy. Now I will never be free from that *lámpara*," the serpent mumbled.

"Make me the richest man in the world," Rico ordered the serpent.

"What have I done?" Bonita cried.

"Too late, *señora*." Rico turned to the serpent. "Well, give me my wish."

The serpent had no other choice and enfolded Rico in his wings. "It shall be true."

Because Rico had turned into the richest man, he bought the clinic and closed it down. He bought the mountain where they had found the gold and built a great house.

Alejandro watched sadly as the doors of his clinic closed.

"Forgive me, my love." Bonita took his hand.

"No, I'm sorry that I didn't tell you about the *lámpara* and the serpent."

Rico grew more powerful and so did his hatred of Alejandro.

"Serpent, bring Bonita to me. That is my wish."

The serpent had to obey. Bonita faded right in front of Alejandro's eyes as if she were a dream.

"Rico!" Alejandro shook his fist in the air.

Jumping into his truck, Alejandro drove to Rico's mountain home, which was well guarded. From a distance, he watched through a window as Bonita sat sobbing.

"What am I to do?" Alejandro put his head between his hands.

"Perhaps I can be of assistance," a familiar voice said.

The serpent sprawled out beside him.

"Rico is your master now. Isn't that the rules?"

"Yes, but where does it say in those rules that I cannot help you as well?"

"*Gracias*, great serpent."

"Rico is too greedy and I hate greed. It toppled my empire." Large tears filled the eyes of the winged serpent. But then he straightened up so tall that he blocked out the moon. "I will make the guards fall asleep while you steal the lamp. It is hidden in a little place under the floor in the living room. Rico has no imagination."

The serpent blew a breath at the guards, and they fell into a deep slumber. Alejandro sneaked into the house and found the loose floorboard and the *lámpara*.

"That's mine," Rico yelled, rushing into the room.

"Not anymore, you evil man," Alejandro replied.

Rico grabbed Bonita, who had run in behind him, and held her tight. "I have your pretty wife. Hand me the *lámpara* and I'll give her back to you."

"Alejandro, don't give it to him. He'll only do more harm," Bonita pleaded. Then she kicked Rico in the shins and ran to her husband.

Quickly, Alejandro rubbed the lamp.

The serpent appeared. "I am so happy it is you, Alejandro."

"Serpent, I wish for things to be the way they were before Rico stole the *lámpara*, and that Rico will never be able to hurt people again."

"My pleasure." The serpent winked.

"No!" shouted Rico.

The serpent folded his wings, and when he unfolded them, Alejandro,

Bonita, and Rico stood before the clinic, which was open. Then Rico was gone in a poof of smelly smoke.

"Serpent, where did you send him?" Bonita said.

"To the top of the world, where it is cold and lonely," the serpent replied. "If his heart ever warms, he shall be able to come home."

"As for my next wish . . ." Alejandro began to say.

Bonita placed her hand on his arm. "My dear husband, please be careful."

Alejandro smiled. "I wish for the serpent to be free of the *lámpara* forever."

The serpent began to cry, tears that turned into blue sapphires when they hit the ground.

117

"Now you can join the other ancient spirits. I have all the riches I need," Alejandro said.

"You are indeed a good man," the serpent said.

Alejandro took his wife's hand. "I have learned that magic is not found in a mysterious *lámpara* or in old treasures, no matter how brightly they shine."

"You are wise for someone who is not hundreds of years old like me. Now, it is time to say goodbye," the serpent said, spreading his blue and green wings. He flew toward the moon.

Alejandro and Bonita watched until the serpent became part of the stars.

They kept the empty *lámpara* on a shelf in their house to remind them that magic was, most of all, in the way they lived their lives.

Belleza y La Bestia

ALWAYS THE SAME.

Nothing changes. The lonely days. The nightly hunt for food. No footsteps to hear but my own.

No visitors come to my house, and any who did would be frightened.

I am no longer a man. *Yo soy La Bestia*. I am the Beast.

My hands are no longer hands, but vicious, deadly claws. My teeth are no longer teeth, but fangs, good for tearing meat and nothing else.

But do not weep for me. This is my fault.

As I watch from my veranda, the night skies turn as black as my animal nose and then give way to thick rain. It was on such a night the old woman came, knocking on my door. Of course, back then, I was handsome, with dark eyes and golden skin. But I was not a good man.

Even when I was a boy, I treated my servants like my toy soldiers, to be pushed around at my whim. I didn't consider their poverty, nor that of the people who worked the land around my large house. I just rode my horse past the Indians and mestizos, and saw nothing but the road ahead.

When I went to mass at the cathedral, the priest's words about love and sharing meant nothing. Land and wealth were all that mattered. People rushed to the dances at my house, and many women smiled at me through their lace mantillas, but I realize now they were mostly smiling at my money.

My country was breaking apart with revolution and chaos. The poor began to shout for land and for change, and the name of Benito Juárez, whom they called the president of Mexico. I did not recognize that rebel government and instead asked Emperor Maximilian to send guards to protect my property. No matter that Maximilian was not Mexican but a puppet of the French. He was royalty. Juárez was just a short Zapotec Indian who dressed in black.

Meanwhile, I spent my days and nights pursuing only my pleasure, so I was in no mood to help a dirty *viejita* at my door.

"*Por favor, señor*, may I come in?" she whined. "It is cold and I am hungry and tired."

"You're not a Juarista—a revolutionary—are you?" I shouted at her.

She shook her head.

"Go to the stable," I ordered, not even looking at her face. "But please don't eat the horses' grain. They are stallions and worth more than you. Now leave me."

How stupid I was.

The *viejita* raised her scrawny arms to the sky, and from her hands flew balls of fire. I began to shake because I realized too late that I had refused help to a *bruja*, a witch of great power.

"*Hombre.*" She pointed a crooked finger at me. "You have no soul, so you will become an animal until you learn what it is to be a man."

Right then, a gigantic owl swooped down, swept up the *bruja* in its claws, and carried her away.

"She is crazy. Nothing will happen," I whispered, and went back inside my house.

That night, I ate my supper and then stretched out on my large bed, waiting for sleep, amused at the empty curse of the *bruja*. "An animal. Ha."

As sudden as breath, a pain crawled over me. I watched helplessly as long, heavy black hairs grew out of my body, each an agony, as if thorns were tearing out of my skin.

"*Dios mío*, save me, save me."

Too late. My prayers were too late.

My nails shot into long, curved claws. In my gilt-framed mirror, I stared at the animal I had become. I had the slitted, yellow eyes of a *gato*. I touched my ears, which were as pointed as a wolf's. My animal nose sniffed. I could smell the night and the scents of wild animals creeping about in it.

I opened my mouth and howled at my carelessness, a howl of desperation.

How long ago was that dreadful night? Months? Years? For me, the days have seemed like years. And each night has been one long hunt for deer in the forest beyond my house to satisfy my hunger.

The *bruja* also put a spell on my household and servants. The servants vanished and the house began to care for itself. Brooms sweep. Beds make themselves, and dishes wash themselves, keeping me all the lonelier.

So I watch the sunset from my veranda, waiting for another day to end.

On this night, however, a man rides a horse toward my house. The man sways with exhaustion as the horse makes its way through the woods. Ashamed of my appearance, I hide, but my broad chest rises with excitement at the sound of a voice and footsteps other than my own.

"House, take care of him," I whisper.

Spying from the shadows, I see the man come through the gates and dismount. He is an Indian and takes small steps, both curious and fearful. The doors of my house open to him. A fine dinner lies before him. He eats hungrily. His clothes are worn and patched, his sombrero beaten and dusty. The old man steps out to my garden and looks in the well, which is also bewitched.

"Show him what he is thinking of," I whisper as I watch, now from the balcony.

The well's water clears and begins to glow. It shows a beautiful young woman searching the roads. She wears a ragged dress but carries herself proudly.

"*Mi* Belleza," the man cries.

Her eyes are as green as the trees of Michoacán. Her hair is black and curly like my animal's mane but shines like the richest silk. Her skin is as tawny as a doe's. She indeed earns her name: Beauty.

"Papá, Papá, where are you?" she calls into the night, searching for her lost father.

"*Mi* Belleza, shall I ever see you again?" The man touches the surface of the water and the image disappears.

• • •

In the morning, the old man rises from the bed he has chosen in my house and heads for the door. He walks toward his horse. But then he stops and gathers a bouquet of marigolds from my garden. The nerve to take my flowers!

A growl comes over me. I leap to his side and he falls to his knees. "You dare to steal from me!" I bellow.

"Please, Don Bestia, don't kill me."

"I gave you everything and yet you steal. What is your name, thief?"

"Diego Hernández López, Don Bestia. I was riding with dispatches to the armies of Presidente Juárez, but I got lost in a storm."

"Why did you want my flowers?" I roar.

"For my daughter, Belleza. She has a beautiful heart, and her laugh

alone can dry a baby's tears. She represents all that is good in these troubling times. I am not rich, but she is my treasure." He hangs his head. "Now I shall never see her or her sisters again."

"Why is that?"

"Because you are going to eat me."

"No, Señor López. You will see her, but I have a bargain for you."

The old man lifts his head.

Putting my claw on his quaking shoulder, I whisper, "I will give you riches, Señor López, enough so you can buy supplies for your pitiful war, but only if . . ."

"Yes?"

"If Belleza promises to stay with me forever—*para siempre*."

The man cries out, "No!"

My voice is calm. "If you do not agree, you must come back to me to die. You may return to your family to tell them about my offer or to say *adiós*. The choice is yours."

"How will I return here, Don Bestia?" the man asks after a long while.

"I will tell your horse the way."

Speaking into his horse's ear, I tell the creature how to bring the man or Belleza back through the deep woods to my house. The horse nods and neighs.

"To show you that I will keep my word, Señor López, I will give you four bags of gold."

I lead the old man to a room where his eyes open wide. We place the bags on his saddle. I stroke the horse's mane. "If you do not send Belleza or return yourself, Señor López, the gold will turn to dust. Now be on your way."

Watching him ride off, I know I will remain a beast until I die. I have done a most selfish thing by asking for his daughter, but I have to meet Belleza.

• • •

Days go slower than ever as I keep watch for Belleza. If her father returns, I tell myself, I will kill him as I promised.

Then, one day, a woman rides toward my house. Tears fill my eyes and they sting.

Belleza gets down off the horse. "Señor Bestia," she calls.

"I am over here. *Bienvenida*, Belleza." Into the light I step.

She draws back. It pains me to see her frightened. I cover my face with my claws. Belleza fights her fear, comes forward, and stares straight at me. How noble she is. Nobler than anyone I ever saw in Maximilian's court.

"I did not want my father to die, so I came to you. Now he has money for the government of Presidente Juárez to fight Maximilian and the French armies that have invaded our country. Yet know this, Señor Bestia: I come with only half a heart, because I will miss my father and sisters. But you have my promise I will stay with you . . . forever." Her mouth trembles.

"Then I shall try to fill the other half of your heart," I say.

Belleza looks at me curiously.

126

"House, treat her like a queen," I command.

"Belleza, everything here is yours. I ask only that you join me for dinner each night."

She nods.

Candles and torches light her way to her room, a large one with a golden bed and a huge closet filled with gowns of silk and satin. For the first time in months, years, I am happy.

For dinner I put on my best clothes of velvet. Belleza wears one of the new gowns. I try not to stare. Even the candles bow to her beauty.

"Do you like your clothes? Are they not lovely?" I ask.

"*Sí*, but many people in our country have only rags to put on their backs. So it is hard for me to enjoy these dresses."

I motion for her to sit at one end of the long table set with only one plate.

"Bestia, why aren't you eating?" she said.

"I will eat later. Please don't wait for me."

Belleza eats delicately and gazes at the surroundings. Then she puts down her fork and fixes her eyes directly on mine. "Why am I here, Bestia?"

I can't lie to her. "Your father's description of you touched me."

"You sound sensitive, but yet you take me away from my family."

Shame burns my cheeks. "I am sorry. I was overpowered by my . . ."

Belleza looks around the grand but silent room. "By your loneliness."

I hang my head, but hearing the truth, I feel that I can deny her nothing—except her freedom.

When I raise my head, she smiles at me. "Bestia, I don't blame you. I would be lonely, too."

Beasts cannot smile, so I just nod.

After dinner, we sit by the fire, and she tells me about the freedom fighters who go into battle against the French. They are armed only with machetes, old weapons, and bravery. She cooked for the men and cared for the wounded. She sings to me of their deaths and their struggles. Her voice is beautiful and strong with her beliefs.

> *"Now we have nothing but hopelessness,*
> *But we shall have freedom,*
> *We shall have victory or death.*
> ¡Viva Juárez!"

Her compassion for others and love of our country move me deeply.

She rises from her chair. "I am tired. I am going to bed."

"Belleza," I say quietly.

She stops.

"Will you marry me?"

Belleza gently shakes her head. "No, Bestia. I do not love you. But I am no longer afraid of you. *Buenas noches.*"

Later, I pass by her bedroom and hear her cry out for her father. Yet the hunt calls to me and I run away from the sounds of her unhappiness.

• • •

Every night she dines while I sit with her. We talk of her life. She grew up poor and uneducated, but considers herself rich because she has her family. She enjoyed taking care of her father and two older sisters, Avaricia and Egoísta, who sound spoiled. On some nights, she tells wonderful, funny stories of ghosts and spells that crackle like the fire. Her voice is as steady as a heartbeat.

When Belleza turns her eyes to me, I immediately cover my face with my claws.

"Don't look at me, Belleza. I am *feo* and I do not want you to be afraid."

With her tiny hands, she pulls my claws away. "We are only afraid of what we don't understand, Bestia. True ugliness can be found only in the hearts of people who hurt others."

Every day, I teach her to read. She learns quickly, picking up each word as a child would a new toy. We sit in the woods together as she reads books on the grass or gathers orange and yellow marigolds. Her beauty makes me feel all the more unhappy.

Each evening after she finishes dinner, I ask her to marry me, and every time, she says, "No, *mi bestia*." But over the many nights, her voice grows friendlier, more trusting.

I am angry at myself for keeping her prisoner, but I can't let her go.

Then one beautiful morning, I find Belleza in the garden. She seems so sad that the flowers have wilted from her gloom.

"Belleza, what is wrong?"

130

"I miss my papá and my sisters. I feel in my heart that something is not right."

"Come with me."

I lead her to the well. "Please show Belleza her family."

The water churns and then stills. The image shows her father on his bed, his face sunken. A priest says words over him. Belleza's sisters hover around the old man, pretending to weep. They have greedy, mean eyes. I know those kinds of eyes very well.

Belleza sinks to her knees. "He is dying. Let me visit. I know I can bring him back to health. *Por favor, mi bestia.*" She takes one of my claws and kisses it. Her tears burn with sincerity on my animal skin.

I agree, although my heart sinks to the bottom of the well. "You can go home, Belleza. But if you do not return in one month . . ."

"*¿Sí?*"

"I will die from loneliness. Now that I have known you, I cannot live without you. The choice is yours, Belleza."

Her eyes turn bright with gratitude. "*Gracias, gracias.* I shall return."

"The horse knows the way."

I load sacks of gold coins onto the horse. "This money will aid your family and your revolution."

She has tears in her eyes, and I am surprised and touched at the sight of them.

"Thank you, *mi bestia*, for your kindness. I will see you in one month."

But her words sound of eternal farewell.

"*Adiós*, Belleza."

As she rides away, I run to the roof and watch her head toward the horizon. She turns and looks back at my house.

I know then that I love her.

With Belleza gone, my heart is like a candle burning down to nothing. My house, which was lonely before, now torments me. I can't stand to hear only my own breathing or my own footsteps. I can still smell her and hear her voice.

Desperate to see her face, I go to the well.

"Please show me Belleza."

The water churns and reveals her two sisters.

"Let's lie to Belleza and tell her that Papá will die without her," Avaricia says, touching the gold coins in the bags. "Then we can use all the money for ourselves."

Egoísta nods. "Yes, we'll keep the silly creature so busy, she will forget about that animal."

"Then the beast will die and we will find his hacienda and take all his gold and live like Empress Carlota."

The sisters laugh and laugh.

The water churns again and shows Belleza walking arm in arm with her father, who is still pale, but stronger.

"I am glad you are better, Papá," she says.

"Must you go back to that beast?"

"If I don't, he will die. I am sure I can visit again. He is not a monster, *mi padre*, but sad and gentle."

Her sisters run up to them.

"You must not leave," Avaricia tells Belleza. "Papá cannot live without you."

"Stay with us a little longer, *hermana*," Egoísta begs. "There is much to do for our cause, for Mexico."

Belleza hesitates a little. "Just for a while, then I must get back."

"No more, no more," I order the well, and its water becomes dark blue.

A cold breeze stirs, and I whisper, "You are free, Belleza, you are free."

My words fly away on the wind.

I stop hunting and eating. But a peacefulness descends on me, one I have never before known, perhaps because freeing Belleza was the first unselfish act of my life.

For most of the day, I sleep, not having the strength for anything else. At night, I drag myself to the place in the garden where Belleza often sat reading books. I no longer smell her. I lie down on the grass and remain there until morning, the sun sliding over my face.

"Belleza," I whisper. With great effort, I lift up my claw, wishing it was a human hand, then rest it on my chest; I can hardly breathe. Still, I am happy knowing Belleza is happy.

I close my eyes.

"Bestia, *por qué*, Bestia?" a familiar voice asks. "Wake up."

My eyes flutter. Belleza has my head on her lap. "*Por favor, por favor, mi bestia*, wake up."

She gives me wine, but the taste is sour and overpowering. "Forgive me,

Bestia. My wicked sisters tricked me into staying longer than I had promised."

I don't have the strength to speak.

"Bestia, I love you," she says. "You are not an animal, but kind and understanding. I will marry you. Can you hear me? Don't leave me."

Her tears fall on my face, and they are like drops of sunlight. My skin feels warm and radiant.

Belleza recoils, frightened. The beast's hair and hide melt off my body and face. I lift my claws to my head and feel human ears, which hear my servants stir inside the house. My muscles find more strength, and I raise my arm into the air. There are fingers and nails, no claws.

"*Gracias*, Belleza, *gracias* for loving me, *gracias* for breaking the curse."

"My love." Belleza takes my hand. "It was you who broke the curse with your love and sacrifice."

"Will you really marry me?" I say.

"*Sí.*"

• • •

And so we are happy together. I've come to know that it is enough in life to have the love of Belleza and our newborn son. I've given most of my wealth to the poor and the cause. I pray for an end to the war, a victory for Benito Juárez, and freedom, democracy, and independence for our people.

For the first time, I am a human being.

Each night, however, I still hear the woods call me to the hunt. But I now no longer have to answer.

135

Emperador's New Clothes

EMPERADOR GÓMEZ WAS THE MOST POPULAR BOY at Emiliano Zapata High School.

He always dressed as if he had just popped out of a teen magazine, from his perfectly gelled spiky hair to the soles of his expensive tennis shoes. Every morning, he took two hours to get dressed, staring at himself in the full-length mirror in his room, using different poses to make sure he was perfect from every angle. He didn't just want to be in style. He wanted to *be* style. He didn't just want to look good. He wanted everyone else to look bad.

Emperador dated the prettiest girls, was president of his class, captain of the basketball team, and the best break-dancer in his part of town. Every year, he was named best dressed and best kisser in the whole school in the yearbook. As a result, his nickname was El Rey, the King.

Even if Emperador's clothes clashed and were ugly, the other students complimented him—otherwise they might be considered uncool.

"You're so fine," girls said as Emperador passed.

"You're *número uno*," the boys said.

"I know, I know," Emperador replied to all compliments.

Because you see, Emperador Gómez was not a nice kid.

Surrounded by his admirers, Emperador always made fun of any student he thought didn't have the right clothes.

No one was safe.

"Look at your shirt," he told Enrique Jiménez in the hall. "It looks like your mama mopped the floor with it."

A group of kids laughed. Enrique laughed too, but it hurt to be insulted by El Rey.

"Those pants ain't working." Emperador wagged a finger at Rubén Vasquez. "I've seen better hanging in a secondhand store."

Rubén hung his head.

"Your jeans are too short," Emperador said to Diane Salazar in study hall. "Are you expecting a flood?"

Diane's cheeks heated up. "You're right, Emperador. I was just hoping nobody would notice. I mean, I hoped *you* wouldn't notice."

"Yeah, right," Emperador said.

"Carmen Vargas, your top is so last year," Emperador told her in the cafeteria in front of everyone, who laughed.

Carmen ran away crying.

"She can't stand to hear the truth." He shrugged his well-dressed shoulders and sat by his friends.

Watching all this was Veronica Campos.

"Don't cry," Veronica told Carmen as she ran past.

"How can I show my face?" Carmen said, heading right to the bathroom to hide out, at least until fifth period.

Veronica put her hands on her hips. "That Emperador can be so mean to people."

Veronica was as kind as Emperador was unkind. She didn't care about what others thought of her clothes and dressed how she wanted.

With each school day, Emperador's ego grew larger and larger until it seemed bigger than the soccer and football fields put together. Now he began to order his friends to dress a certain way.

"Arturo, go to the mall and get that red shirt, man. The girls will go crazy for you."

"Thanks for the tip," Arturo said, and headed straight to the mall after school, even though the shirt would cost him all the money he had.

"Yolanda, you need to buy a new skirt. The one you're wearing is totally 1990s," Emperador complained.

139

"Oh, yes I will buy one, Emperador. You have such good taste. You're the man."

Even the teachers and the principal, Mr. Sandoval, could not escape his fashion criticism.

"Mr. Sandoval, your vest reminds me of my grandma's rug, and if your tie was any wider, I could use it for a blanket," Emperador said with a sneer.

Mr. Sandoval began to perspire. "Better get to class" was all that he could manage to say.

Boys began to dress just like Emperador and the girls dressed like his girlfriend, Lita Méndez, who was a cheerleader, prom queen, and as friendly as a pop math quiz.

Veronica tried to convince people that they shouldn't listen to Emperador, but just be themselves.

"But, Veronica, if we don't dress like Lita, no one will like us," Sophia Otero said as they walked down the hall.

"Emperador runs this school," added Santiago Espinoza.

Veronica leaned against the lockers and sighed with frustration.

Then she had an idea—an idea as delicious as the macaroni-and-nacho-cheese served every Friday in the cafeteria.

During lunch, Veronica sat by Hector "the Mouth" Trujillo. He was called the Mouth because he couldn't keep a secret and anything told to him was instantly passed around the school faster than having it announced on the loudspeaker.

"Hey, Hector, did you hear that a world-famous fashion designer is coming right here to Emiliano Zapata High School?"

"No, I didn't hear that," Hector said.

"And the designer is choosing one student to do a photo shoot wearing his clothes for a national magazine," Veronica whispered to him while he ate his hamburger. "But please don't tell anyone."

"I won't tell." Hector shook his head.

In an hour, the news had spread from the gymnasium to the office. Emperador was among the first to hear.

"You know they'll pick me," he told his friends, and they nodded like geese.

The designer clothes became the talk of the entire school. No one questioned who would be selected to wear them. It must be Emperador.

Veronica was ready for the next step. She was sitting next to Hector the Mouth in chemistry when she told him, "I just heard that Emperador has been chosen to wear the designer clothes for the photo shoot."

Hector spread the word by the time second period buzzed in.

Emperador walked down the halls as if he had known it all along. "First a magazine, and then who knows how far I'll go," he bragged to his followers.

Anticipation ran as high as the flagpole in front of the school.

The day came for Veronica to put the rest of her plan into action.

First she called Mr. Sandoval and pretended to represent the designer. Then she asked the principal for a special assembly so Emperador could preview the designer clothes before the entire school. Mr. Sandoval agreed because he also was intimidated by Emperador. Then, while the school secretary was busy photocopying school menus, Veronica clicked on the loudspeaker.

"The designer clothes have arrived and are ready for preview," she said, disguising her voice. "Will Emperador Gómez please report to room C-7 before lunch."

A cheer was heard around the building.

Emperador arrived at the door to C-7 right before the lunch bell. He entered, but no one was there. Then the phone rang in the room and Emperador answered it.

"Emperador Gómez." Veronica lowered her voice and held her nose to sound like a snobby adult.

"Yes."

"This is Maxine Delgado. I represent the famous designer Victor Ropa, who would like you to try out his new line of clothes before showing them in New York. We heard you were just the man."

"You made a good choice," Emperador said.

"I'm sure we did. I couldn't get there today, but you will find the clothes in the closet. Put me on the speaker phone so I can talk with you," Veronica said.

Emperador strolled to the closet, ready for greatness. He unzipped the clothes bag and found nothing but hangers.

"Where are they?" Emperador said, a bit confused, then angry. What if

someone had stolen the clothes and wore them before he got a chance to make them famous?

"The clothes are there, Mr. Gómez, but they are so beautiful and fashionable that only the coolest people can see them."

"I don't see them," Emperador blurted out.

"Perhaps we have selected the wrong person to represent us in a magazine. You are apparently not cool."

The words hit Emperador like a wet taco in the face.

He faked a laugh. "I was only kidding you. These are the baddest clothes I've ever seen."

"Thank you. How do you like the colors?"

"They are terrific!"

"How about the fabric?"

Emperador felt air between his fingers. "Silky and soft."

"And the fit?"

"Hold on." He got undressed down to his boxers, which were covered with pictures of chili peppers and the words HOW HOT AM I? across the behind. Carefully, Emperador took the invisible shirt and pants off the hanger and put them on. He slipped into the unseen socks and shoes. Then he squinted hard at himself in the full-length mirror. After a while, he thought he started to see the clothes.

"These are the greatest clothes I have ever worn. I've never looked so good," he told the voice on the speaker phone.

145

"Then please show them to your fellow students and let us know what people think, Mr. Gómez."

"Sure thing."

"Mr. Gómez, please tell the principal you are ready. Good luck," Veronica said.

Emperador called the principal. "Mr. Sandoval, I am ready. Be sure to tell everybody that only the coolest people can see these clothes."

The principal clicked on the loudspeaker. "Everyone will now meet in the auditorium to see the designer clothes modeled by our one and only Emperador. And I'm told that only the coolest people will be able to see them. That is all."

Students left their classrooms and herded into the auditorium. They talked with excitement. This was the biggest thing to happen since the football team had won state the year before.

Peeking out from behind the curtain, Emperador made sure the crowd was seated. A spotlight flashed on. The curtains parted.

He stepped onto the stage. Of course, he was really wearing nothing but his chili-pepper boxers.

The auditorium was quiet for a second. Then everyone applauded because they didn't want to be considered uncool.

"You look fabulous!" girls cheered. "We love your pants."

"And your shirt is so happening," another kid called out.

"Those shoes will start a new style!"

"*¡Número uno, El Rey!*" the students shouted.

Emperador's chest grew with pride and ego as he strutted across the stage, even turning around to show the back of his outfit.

Standing in front of the stage, Veronica couldn't believe what she was hearing. They were cheering. They weren't supposed to be cheering. They were supposed to see Emperador for what he was: a guy with no clothes on. She scratched her head. Where had her plan gone wrong? Would no one speak the truth? Was no one brave enough? Well, she would speak up, even though people would probably laugh at her for not being cool enough to see those clothes.

Just as she was about to open her mouth, a tiny freshman named Anita Peña who had transferred from another school stood up. She was bewildered by all the fuss over this kid onstage in the goofy underwear.

"THAT BOY DON'T HAVE NO CLOTHES ON!" Anita proclaimed. "ALL HE HAS ARE BOXER SHORTS!"

Her shout reverberated around the auditorium.

Emperador stopped in the middle of the stage.

The faces of the other students reddened with doubt, and then they snickered. Then they laughed full-out at the sight of Emperador, strutting around in his chili-pepper shorts.

"That style is out of style," one girl remarked.

"Where did you get those pathetic underpants?" yelled a boy.

" 'How hot are you?' More like, 'How cold are you?' " another student called.

Almost faint from being laughed at, Emperador realized that he was in-

deed naked—except for his boxers—and ran back to room C-7. He vowed right on the spot that he would no longer judge anyone by what they wore. Clothes—no matter how "in" or "out"—did not make a difference. It was who was in them.

Veronica told her story to the principal, but didn't get detention. She also confessed to Emperador that she was the one behind the trick, and admitted to feeling a little guilty.

"You shouldn't feel bad," he said. "I deserved it for all the times I laughed at other people."

Soon, Emperador was no longer called El Rey, but El Corazón, because he showed others that he had a king-size heart.

149

The Three Chicharrones

PAPÁ CHICHARRÓN SMILED at his three sons.

Each had curly black hair, small dark eyes, tiny ears, and round, round stomachs, just like their father.

"Pereza, Gordo, and Astuto, it's time for you to go into the world and make your fortunes."

He handed them each little bags. "You'll receive the same number of pesos I received from my *papá* when I was your age."

They opened their bags and found two hundred coins.

"Can't we stay here a little longer, Papá?" drawled Pereza, yawning, for he was lazy.

"This is impossible. How can we make our way in the world like this?" whined Gordo, who always looked for the quickest way to everything.

"I'll do my best, Papá," said Astuto, who always worked hard.

"With two hundred pesos and a lot of work, I did well for myself." Their father spread his arms out, indicating his large house. "Now, get packed, *hijos*."

The next morning, the Chicharrones were ready to set out.

"Don't be greedy like a *cerdo*." Their father grunted his advice. "And this is the most important thing to remember: Watch for the wolf at the door. He will try to take all you have, but you won't know it until you have nothing left."

"What?" replied Pereza, who had only half listened, while Gordo recounted his money.

"*Gracias* for the useful words, Papá," Astuto said.

And so the brothers hugged and bade farewell to each other and their father. They got into their cars and drove off in three different directions.

Pereza hadn't gone very far when he saw a small piece of land for sale at 120 pesos. On the land was a bale-mountain of straw. He said to himself, "A house of *paja* does seem foolish, but I can build it in no time and then take a nap."

He bought the land and built his house, which he called the Casa de Paja, and indeed, the work did not take long. Pereza slept for the rest of the day, too lazy to spend his other pesos.

Meanwhile, Gordo had traveled a little farther down his road when he saw a parcel of land for sale at 150 pesos, which came with a gigantic pile of piñon-tree sticks.

152

"Sticks are a good start," he told himself. "With the rest of the money, I can gamble and make more money so I can have a big fine house. I can't wait too long to get rich."

Gordo closed the deal on the land and built his house of piñon sticks. As soon as he finished what he called Palacio Piñon, he got in his car and headed off to build the rest of his fortune at cards.

Astuto drove the farthest, stopping only when he spotted the exact land he wanted. The property had a nice view of the valley and included a tower of adobe bricks. The land cost 220 pesos, so he sold his car to make up the difference.

Taking his time, Astuto built his house of adobe. He didn't mind the sweat and toil because he knew he would end up with a strong home. When he was finally done, Astuto searched for a job.

Meanwhile, at the Casa de Paja, Pereza had just finished taking another nap.

"Maybe *mañana* I'll start looking for work. But it's too nice of a day for that. I think I'll go fishing instead. I can sleep a little as I wait for a bite."

Just then came a *rap-tap-tap* on the door.

Pereza peered out his window.

"Let me introduce myself. I'm Dinero Martínez. And I'm going to make you rich."

Dinero Martínez was tall and skinny, with big ears and eyes that looked not merely hungry to make a deal, but famished. He wore a hairy gray suit

153

and carried a big black briefcase. Parked out front was his jalapeño-green sports car.

Pereza opened the front door a little. "Do I have to do any work to get rich?"

"Not at all, young *señor*. I'll give you top peso for your house and land—top peso I say, and you don't have to lift a fingernail except to sign." Dinero was smooth as his shiny car and offered double what Pereza had paid in the first place.

"*Bueno*." Pereza yawned.

The ink wasn't even dry on the papers when Dinero's eyes turned hard as rusty coins. "Chicharrón, you must leave. There's soon going to be a huff and a *soplo*, and down goes your silly *casa*. Just look over there."

A bulldozer rumbled along.

Pereza was hardly out of his straw house before the machine chugged and churned and Casa de Paja was flat.

"Foolish Chicharrón, you would have gotten five times more for this land if you weren't so lazy. But I caught you napping." Dinero laughed and laughed as he tacked up a sign: FUTURE SITE OF A NEW HOTEL.

"No matter," Pereza said with a shrug. "I have money. But all this dealing has made me tired." He drove away, looking for a good place to take a nap.

A few days later, Gordo was busy planning a party for his gambling friends when he heard a knock.

Dinero Martínez was at the door.

"I'm going to make you rich," Dinero said.

Gordo's eyes became wide.

Dinero did more of his smooth-talking, and soon Gordo was signing on the dotted line. All the while, Gordo told himself that he would take the money and place larger bets to get rich even faster.

After Gordo sold the land, Dinero bellowed, "Bring on the bulldozer!"

Along came the machine, and down went the Piñon Palacio in a huff and a *soplo*.

"Chicharrón, you could have gotten a lot more pesos. Now it's too late, so get off my land," Dinero ordered Gordo, who started packing his car.

"Gordo!" he heard someone call.

Up the road, Pereza was walking with a suitcase in hand.

"What happened to your car?" Gordo asked.

"Someone stole all my money when I fell asleep by the side of the road, and I had to sell my car to buy food," Pereza said, rubbing his feet. "Ah, I see that you've met Dinero Martínez."

"He just showed up at my door," Gordo replied. "Never mind, Brother. Get in my car. We'll go to the racetrack and win big, then we'll buy even more land."

The brothers turned for a last look and saw a sign go up where Gordo's house had once stood: COMING SOON: NEW CASINO.

But Dinero Martínez wasn't through with the Chicharrones. A few days later, he showed up at the house of Astuto.

"*Buenas tardes*, young *señor*. I am ready to make you a great offer on your land and house." Dinero straightened his tie.

Astuto listened because he was polite. He also smiled because he knew what his land was worth.

"Thank you, Señor Martínez, but I am not interested in selling," Astuto said.

Dinero upped his offer.

Astuto felt deep down in his pudgy stomach that this Martínez in the hairy gray suit was trying to cheat him.

"Again, no thanks," the brother said.

Dinero's eyes became red slits of anger. "You are making a mistake, Chicharrón."

"That may be," Astuto replied, "but you are the one leaving empty-handed."

Dinero got in his sports car and zoomed away.

From the other direction came Pereza and Gordo, walking with their suitcases. They had lost all their money betting and had had to sell Gordo's car for food.

"*¡Hermanos!*" Astuto called out happily.

At supper, Gordo and Pereza told their brother how they had failed to listen to their father's advice and had lost their homes to a wolf who showed up at the door.

"I deserved what I got," Pereza said. "I was too lazy to keep my land or money."

"Ay, yi, yi." Gordo slapped his head. "I wanted to take the fast road to a good life. I gambled and lost."

Then and there, Pereza promised to work hard and Gordo vowed never to make another wager.

"No, my brothers, you haven't lost everything. We have each other," Astuto said. "We will live together."

"But what about Dinero Martínez?" Gordo said.

"He doesn't look like the type to give up so easy," Pereza added.

Astuto grinned. "We are the Chicharrones, and we can handle him if we work together."

Gordo, Pereza, and Astuto laughed and settled down for a nice evening before the fire, snacking on pork rinds and salsa.

The next day, Dinero warned the brothers that Astuto's land was located in a flood plain and would be filled with water when it stormed.

Astuto wouldn't sell.

The next day, Dinero told the brothers that a freeway was going to be built right through their land. He would take it off their hands for more than the freeway department would ever pay.

"No, *gracias,*" Astuto replied.

Dinero returned and advised the brothers that the house was in the path of several tornadoes known to hit at springtime, so they would be better off selling than being swirled away.

The brothers wouldn't budge.

"CHICHARRONES!" Dinero bellowed with frustration, because this was the first time in his sleazy career that he could not close a deal. "Some-day my bulldozer *will* come with a huff and a *soplo*, and well, you know the rest . . ."

"How do we get rid of this pest?" Gordo asked that night at supper.

"I have a plan," Astuto said.

"Of course you do," Pereza replied. "That's why we love you."

The following morning, Gordo and Pereza were out working in the garden. They talked loud to each other because they knew Dinero was listening around the corner.

"I'm really looking forward to going to the fiesta in town tonight," Gordo said, picking corn.

"We're all going to have a good time," Pereza said, plucking tomatoes off the vine.

"Ah-ha!" Dinero said to himself. "I'll burn down the house while they are gone. Then they'll *have* to sell the land to me."

Wearing their best clothes, the brothers started walking toward town.

When they were out of sight, Dinero sneaked up to the adobe house. He lit a match and was ready to start the fire when a bright light shone in his face.

"Hands up," a deep voice commanded.

Dinero turned around to see the Chicharrones with County Sheriff Sánchez.

"You've been cheating folks long enough, Dinero Martínez," Sheriff

Sánchez said. "I'm going to see to it that you lose your license to do business. You won't be able to sell a *ratón* to a *gato*."

"Wait, let's talk," Dinero pleaded, using his best salesman voice. "I know about some great land in Florida."

The sheriff shook his head and led him away. "Say *adiós*."

Dinero knew he hadn't made a deal. "*Adiós*, Chicharrones."

"*Adiós*, Dinero." The Chicharrones waved goodbye.

After working hard and saving their pesos, the brothers decided to go into business for themselves. They started Residencias Chicharrones, which were homes for those just starting out in life. The houses they built weren't made of straw or piñon sticks, but of adobe bricks that were sturdy and would last.

The Sleeping Beauty

(as told by the *bruja* who cast the spell)

I<small>T ALL STARTED</small> at Rosa's *quinceañera*.

For weeks, the whole town did nothing but talk about Rosa's up-coming fifteenth birthday celebration and how she was going to have more than one dozen *damas* in pretty blue dresses and an equal number of *chambelanes* to escort them, all handsome and good dancers.

"Everyone was invited," I told my pet owl, Pluma. "Everyone but me. People don't think that a witch has feelings. But I have plenty, let me tell you, and they're hurt. And I'm not ashamed to admit that when a *bruja's* feelings are hurt, she can hold a grudge for a long time."

"*¿Tú? ¿Tú? ¿Tú?*" Pluma hooted.

At my home outside of town, I waited each day for an invitation to the *quinceañera*. None came, which didn't surprise me at all. Rosa and I went to school together. But she and her friends always ignored or laughed at me. I had no parents, my best friend was an owl, and I knew the *bruja's* art for making mischief. That made me different. And being different made me lonely.

The day before the birthday party, I went to the big house of Rosa's *padre* and *madre* and peeked in a window at all the preparations. Rosa was trying on her fancy white dress of satin and lace. She was a pretty girl, I had to admit, with great big eyes of brown and skin the color of perfect wood.

"I'm so excited," Rosa told her mother. "Don't I look beautiful? Don't I look like a princess? Don't I look like I walked right out of a storybook?"

"Oh, brother," I said.

Her mother kissed her cheek. "Yes, you are beautiful. We are all happy, and everyone has been invited, except the old *bruja* in the desert."

"Old! I'm not old," I whispered to my owl. "Rosa and I are the same age. I just didn't have a *mamá* and *papá* to spoil me, because I was an orphan."

"*¿Huérfana? ¿Huérfana? ¿Huérfana?*" Pluma replied.

"Rosa," her mother said, "maybe we should invite her after all. *Brujas* have tempers."

"No, I don't want her to come. She's weird," Rosa said, brushing her thick hair. "I don't want anything to spoil my *quinceañera*. I deserve the best of everything."

When they left the room, I climbed through the window and lifted a few strands of Rosa's hair off her brush. In case I wanted to cast a spell on Rosa, I needed a little piece of her.

The day of the *quinceañera* arrived and still no invitation. I headed to town. Rosa's house was filled with laughter and music. I hated music because it reminded me of people having fun. No one believed that a witch should have any fun. It's not that *brujas* want to be mean; it's just that people don't give us a chance. Certainly, Rosa's family didn't give me the chance to show that I can laugh, dance, and be nice.

"Stop feeling sorry for yourself," I scolded myself.

Self-pity was replaced by anger when the three meddlesome *madrinas*, who had a little magic of their own, showed up at the party.

"They asked those godmothers but not me. Now I'm really mad," I told my owl.

"*¿Uno, dos, tres?*" Pluma asked.

Inside, Rosa and the guests danced, boys circling her. I covered my ears. The music made my head hurt.

The food came out and I covered my nose. At last, it was time for the gifts. Rosa received a pile of them—rosaries, rings, dresses. The whole place hushed when the *madrinas* presented their gifts, because everyone knew they were going to be pretty good.

"I wish for *mi ahijada* Rosa a long life and happiness," said Madrina Sopita.

"Ahhhhh," the crowd said.

"Bahhhh," I said.

"*Sí, sí, sí,*" my owl said.

"And I wish for *mi ahijada* to have a handsome man to be her husband," said Madrina Vivita.

"Ahhhh," the crowd said.

"Whooo, whooo, whooo," my owl said.

"I can't take any more of this," I told Pluma, and swept into the house. People crossed themselves like crazy.

"I'm very annoyed that I wasn't invited to this party," I announced, pacing up and down and waving my hands, which really scared them. "You hurt my feelings."

The crowd whimpered. Rosa's *madre* and *padre* clung to her.

"Here's my gift to Rosa." I smiled. I can be very wicked when I want to be. "On her eighteenth birthday, I wish that Rosa will prick her finger on a spinning wheel. And fall asleep—forever." The words spilled out like my anger.

Cries went up to the ceiling.

"*Señorita*, we beg you," said Rosa's parents.

"Too late. You should have invited me." I stormed out, pleased with myself.

"*Buenooo, buenooo, buenooo,*" my owl said.

I started home. Then I slowed my steps. Maybe I shouldn't have been so

169

mean. I decided to return to the house. I just wanted to watch Rosa cry. Since this was the worst spell I had ever cast, I actually wasn't exactly sure it would even work. Usually, I give people upset stomachs or turn their hair purple.

Back at the house, Rosa *was* crying, her parents were weeping, and the guests were moaning.

"*¡Un momento!*" shouted Madrina Conchita.

The room quieted.

"I still have my gift for Rosa."

"Uh-oh," I whispered to my owl. "I forgot about her."

"Nooooo, noooo, nooo," he replied.

"I wish that Rosa will not sleep forever. I wish that she will sleep only until she is awakened by true love's kiss."

Rosa put her hands on her hips, tapped her small foot, and pursed her red lips. "What? Why couldn't you have broken the *bruja*'s spell completely?"

"She's powerful," Madrina Sopita replied. "Isn't that better than sleeping forever?"

Rosa thought about it and decided it was indeed better.

"I hereby order all the spinning wheels in the land to be burned," commanded Rosa's father, a powerful man.

"*Sí, patrón,*" the workers replied.

"Let's not waste a good *quinceañera*," Rosa said, signaling for the band to start playing. The party continued.

As I walked back home, the sky was lit with fires from all the spinning wheels being burned.

"So those *madrinas* think they can outsmart me, eh?" I told Pluma. "I'll wait and get my revenge."

"Ho, ho, ho," my owl said.

Years go fast if you are waiting for revenge, and they did for me. I spent the days reading books, practicing spells, and learning new ones because I had no friends and that is all I had to do with my time. One morning, I looked in the mirror, combed my hair, and smiled.

I had grown pretty.

Then I became depressed. "Who's going to see me anyway? Who will fall in love with a *bruja*? I should wish for a good-looking man, too," I told Pluma.

"Guapo, guapo, guapo," said my owl.

Before I knew it, it was Rosa's eighteenth birthday.

This time, there was no fiesta. Instead, her mother and father locked her in a room all day so she couldn't get out and somehow find a spinning wheel. I peeked in their window.

"We'll celebrate her *cumpleaños* tomorrow," her mother said.

"We'll eat well and laugh at that *bruja*," her father added. "Let's see to the food."

As they left, I snickered quietly. They didn't know I had hidden away the very last spinning wheel in the whole county. It was very heavy as I dragged it up the stairs to a room next to Rosa's. Then I pulled out a set of keys that would open anything and unlocked Rosa's door.

"Rosa," I called in my sweetest voice. "Rosa."

Besides being vain and mean, Rosa also was nosy. She just had to find out who had beckoned her. Meanwhile I sat, spinning wool into thread. I hated spinning. The wool made me sneeze. She didn't come.

"Rooooosa," I called again.

Soon, the door opened and in she walked, even more beautiful than the years before. She didn't recognize me because I had disguised myself as an old woman.

"Were you calling me, *viejita*?" Rosa said.

I batted my skimpy eyelashes. "Yes."

"Do I know you? What are you doing here?" Rosa said.

"Spinning."

"I thought my father ordered all these burned." Rosa applied another coat of lipstick.

This might be harder than I thought.

"Ah, this is a special spinning wheel. It spins gold," I answered with a good comeback.

"That sounds like a kid's story."

"Don't believe me? Why not try it?"

Rosa leaned in and stared at the spinning wheel. "No. I don't want to. It would be work. I don't want to break a nail. I've just had them done."

"You're right—it is too difficult to understand. Only the smartest peo-ple can spin gold."

Rosa stepped forward. "I'm very smart. Move aside, old lady."

Of course, she pricked her finger.

"Uh-oh," she said before she plopped down on the floor.

"*Sueña, sueña, sueña,*" my owl called.

Rosa was snoring loudly. Even though I got what I wanted, I didn't feel as happy as I thought I would. Being a witch is just not as rewarding as it sounds.

"That was too easy," I said, petting my owl's fine feathers. "Let's go home, Pluma."

As I reached for the door, the three *madrinas* rushed in, bumping into one another.

"Too late, too late, too late," my owl hooted.

"*Dios mío,*" the three women said, seeing Rosa on the floor.

"You evil old *bruja.*" Madrina Vivita wagged a fat finger in my direc-tion.

"I'm not old," I replied.

"Just because you're unhappy, you want everyone else to be unhappy," Madrina Conchita said.

"I am happy—happy to be rid of this spoiled girl."

The *madrinas* huddled. They turned back to me with a plan.

"We're going to put a spell on this house so no one will know of your bad deeds," Madrina Sopita said. "*Everyone* will sleep until Rosa's true love arrives."

"Ha!" I said. "You're going to have to wait a long time to find anyone stupid enough to fall in love with Rosa."

They ignored me, prayed a little, and burned some special herbs that smelled of soap and *sopa*. Soon the entire household was asleep. The three *madrinas* were pleased with themselves.

I rolled up my sleeves. "Well then, I'm going to make very sure that her true love has a real tough time getting in here."

From my pocket I drew my special oils that smelled of scorpions and *cucarachas*. I held my nose and rubbed the oil on the walls. The ground grumbled as giant cactuses grew all around with thorns as big as swords.

"Let someone try to get past these *nopales grandes*," I said with a laugh.

"*Ay*," the *madrinas* sang in sad harmony.

One year passed, and I often walked by Rosa's house to check on whether the cactus plants were still thriving. They were. Yet I grew even lonelier because everyone else was asleep.

A crow who liked to gossip told me that the *madrinas* were out trying to recruit rich men to cut their way through the cactus, but none were brave enough to try.

Then one morning, as I walked past the house with Pluma on my shoulder, I spotted a handsome young man riding a horse toward Rosa's

175

house. His face was strong as a wall, but also tender. He was as princely as any gentleman, although his clothes were humble.

"*Hola, señorita.* Is this the house with the sleeping beauty inside?" he said.

"Yes, but aren't you frightened of those big cactus plants surrounding the place?" I said.

He shook his head. "I grew up in the desert and I've seen some even bigger than these. Excuse me now. I'll try to see if the stories are true."

"Good luck," I told him, but didn't know why I said it.

"Thank you," he said.

His smile warmed me. At that moment, I knew why I had wished him luck.

"What's your name?" I called as he rode toward Rosa's house.

"Pepe. And you?"

No one had ever asked me before. "Maricela." The word sounded odd on my tongue.

"Pretty name for a pretty girl." He smiled again and rode on.

"Pepe." I repeated his name.

I followed on foot. When Pepe reached the house, he pulled out the largest machete I had ever seen. He took a deep breath and whacked away at the cactuses. The thorns flew this way and that, but Pepe continued on.

"How handsome and courageous he is," I said to my owl.

"Bravo, bravo, bravo," the owl agreed.

At last, Pepe cut his way through and reached the courtyard, where he found everyone asleep. I followed as he searched the rooms, looking for Rosa.

"He called her a sleeping beauty—what a dumb name," I told my owl.

After much searching, Pepe found the room where Rosa slept. I watched from the doorway.

Dressed in a lacy white gown and wearing her shiny *quinceañera* crown, Rosa *was* beautiful, mostly because she was asleep and not talking.

Pepe approached her slowly, taking tiny steps as if not to wake her.

"Qué bonita," he whispered.

Envy squeezed my heart.

"I have heard that you will awaken with true love's kiss," he told the snoring Rosa. "I will give you that kiss."

A tear traveled down my cheek. I touched it.

"Oh, no," I told my owl. "I'm crying, and the tears are taking away my *bruja* powers."

"Boo, hoo, hoo," the owl said.

Pepe bent down on one knee and kissed Rosa's lips gently. I touched my own, pretending his *beso* was for me, sweet as sunshine.

Rosa's eyes fluttered and opened. Pepe smiled.

Rosa sat up, frowned, and yelled. "Well, it took you long enough to get here! Do you know how long I've been sleeping? Look at my dress! It's wrinkled. Look at me! I'm all dusty!"

"Sorry," Pepe replied, a bit disappointed at this reception.

Rosa got to her feet. In other rooms, I could hear her family stirring.

Rosa stared at Pepe and his patched pants and worn shirt. "You're not rich, are you?"

"No, I'm a farmer."

She shook cobwebs off her crown. "We'll have to get you new clothes if you're going to marry me. I'm rich, you know."

"I'm proud of being a farmer." Pepe stood tall.

"But you'll like being rich much better," Rosa said.

"Leave him alone." I dashed into the room. "Pepe is good and strong and brave."

Pepe smiled.

Rosa's face twisted with fury. "It's you . . . the *bruja* who cast this horrible sleeping spell."

"You don't have to worry anymore," I said. "I've lost my magic to do harm. I really didn't want to be bad in the first place. It's just that no one ever gave me the chance to be nice or do good. They always thought that just because I was different, I was evil."

"Lost your powers, eh?" Rosa screamed. "I'll have my father send you to prison for making me sleep so long. Just think of all the parties I've missed. Good thing I still have my beauty, or you'd really be in trouble."

"Go ahead. Send me to jail. I just don't want to hear you whine," I said.

"Wait." Pepe stepped up to me. "I think I have found my true love."

"You mean *me*, don't you?" Rosa yelled.

"No, I mean her," Pepe replied, and took my hand. "Maricela, I would love to show you my farm."

"I would love to see it, Pepe," I said.

"Hold on! This is not how this *cuento* is supposed to end," Rosa complained.

"I did my part, *señorita*," Pepe told Rosa. "You're awake, and I hope you live happy ever after."

Rosa's mouth hung wide open in shock, which is how I'll always remember her.

Outside the house, Pepe gave the kiss of true love to me! As he did, goodness and kindness awakened in me after a long sleep.

Glossary

abuelita: affectionate form of *abuela*, grandmother

adiós: goodbye, farewell

ahijada: goddaughter

¡Allá está!: There she is!

arroyo: creek

arroz: rice

astuto: astute, crafty

avaricia: greed

basura: trash

belleza: beauty

beso: kiss

bestia: beast

bienvenida: welcome

blanca: white

bonita: pretty (girl)

bruja: witch

buenas noches: good night

buenas tardes: good afternoon

bueno: good

buenos días: good morning, good day

caballo: horse

cacaoteros: cacao bean vendors

cacto: cactus

café: coffee

calabaza: pumpkin, gourd

carnitas: pork dish

casa: house

casa dulce: sweet house

cena: supper

cerdo: pig

chambelanes: male escorts at a *quinceañera*

chicharrones: pork rinds

chiquilla: little girl

cielo, el: heaven

cocinero: chef

comida: meal

¿Cómo está?: How are you?

conejo: rabbit

corazón: heart

cucarachas: cockroaches

cuento: tale

cuervo: crow

cumpleaños: birthday

curandera: healer

damas: ladies (used to refer to the female attendants at a *quinceañera*)

dame: give me

¡Dame mi dinero!: Give me my money!

Día de los Muertos, El: The Day of the Dead

dientes: teeth

dinero: money

Dios mío: My God

¿Dónde estás?: Where are you?

egoísta: egotist

emperador: emperor

entra: enter

esposo: husband

estúpida: stupid (girl)

feo: ugly

flauta: flute

frijoles: beans

gaitero: piper

gato: cat

giganta: giantess

gordo: fat

gracias: thank you

guapo: handsome

hermana: sister

hermano: brother

hierbas: herbs

hija/hijo: daughter/son

hijos: children

hola: hello

hombre: man

huérfana: orphan

huevo: egg

jefe, el: the chief, the boss

lámpara: lamp

lazo: lasso

lobo: wolf

madrasta: stepmother

madre: mother

madrina: godmother

malo: evil

mañana: tomorrow

mariachi: a type of Mexican street musician

menudo: a spicy stew made with hominy and tripe

mercado: market

mi/mis: my

mira: look

mi nombre es: my name is

molcajete: Mexican type of stone bowl used as a mortar with a pestle

momento: moment

Mucho gusto: It's a pleasure to meet you

muerta: dead

mujer: woman

nada: nothing

nieta: granddaughter

nieves: snow

niños: children

nopales: type of cactus

número uno: number one

octli: an alcoholic drink also known as
pulque

ojos: eyes

orejas: ears

padre: father

paja: straw

palacio: palace

paloma blanca: white dove

pan: bread

pan dulce: a type of sweet bread

panadería: bakery

para siempre: forever

patrón: boss

pereza: sloth, laziness

piñon: pine nut

plateado: silvery

pluma: feather

pobrecitos: poor little ones

pollo: chicken

por favor: please

¿Por qué?: Why?

pozole: a spicy soup made of beef and
hominy

qué: what a, how (used in exclamations)

queso: cheese

quinceañera: a festive traditional
party when a girl turns fifteen

rancherita: female rancher

rancho: ranch

rápido: quick

ratón: mouse

rey: king

roja: red

ropa: clothes

señor: sir, Mr.

Señor, el: God; the Lord

señora: ma'am, Mrs.

señorita: Miss

sí: yes

silencio: silence

sombra: shadow

sopa: soup

soplo: a puff of air/wind

suavecito: smooth one

sueña: dream

Tengo hambre: I'm hungry

toro: bull

tú: you

uno, dos, tres: one, two, three

vaca: cow

Vámonos: Let's go

vaqueritos: little cowboys

vaqueros: cowboys

venga: come here

verdad: true

viejita / viejito: old woman/
old man

185

Virgen de Guadalupe, La: the Virgin Mary, so called after she miraculously appeared to an Indian in Mexico in 1531, which led to the conversion to Christianity of much of Mexico's population

y: and

The character names in the story "El Día de los Muertos" are taken from Aztec legend. Here is a pronunciation guide:

Huitzilopochtli: weet-zil-oh-POHCH-tlee
Miccailhuitontli: mee-ky-eel-wee-TOHNT-tlee
Mictecacihuatl: mik-teh-kah-kee-WAH-tl
Nochehuatl: noh-chay-WAH-tl
Xochiyotl: shoh-chee-YOH-tl

And note that Tenochtitlán (tay-nawk-teet-LAHN) was the Aztec name for Mexico City when it was the capital of their empire.